Take the Heat

Skye Warren
Pam Godwin
Cynthia Rayne
Sheri Savill
Shoshanna Evers
Candy Quinn
Tamsin Flowers
Elizabeth Coldwell
Audrey Lusk
Trent Evans
Giselle Renarde

Warning

This book contains explicit language, sex and violence. There are no rules here. Just dark and twisted characters coming out to play. Not intended for those under eighteen or those uncomfortable with the subject matter.

Contents

The Magnolia Hotel by Skye Warren	1
Unlawful Seduction by Pam Godwin	29
Captivated by Cynthia Rayne	61
Slipknot by Sheri Savill	85
This Might Hurt a Bit by Shoshanna Evers	103
The Bombshell by Candy Quinn	123
Playing with Fire by Tamsin Flowers	147
Disposing of Donnie by Elizabeth Coldwell	171
Surprise Witness by Audrey Lusk	189
Last Day by Trent Evans	209
Acquitted by Giselle Renarde	237

THE MAGNOLIA HOTEL
SKYE WARREN

I COULD HAVE loved the Magnolia Hotel.

With its vertical marquee sign and tarnished brass fixtures, the old building stood testament to a different time. I'd played in the chipped courtyard as a child, imagining swanky parties in the salon and glamorous couples in the rooms above.

But I had never imagined that my playmate would later buy the hotel. I never imagined my playmate would turn into a monster, either. That was the boon of childhood—its sweet, myopic vision.

I wasn't a child anymore, and I could see the building clearly for what it was: a crumbling facade for a criminal enterprise. Two beefy men stood like sentinels at the double doors with their stained-glass-window inlays. One gave me a quick nod, allowing entrance.

A swirl of dust motes met me in the dim hallway. I paused, taking a deep breath of stale air. I thought I even smelled the soft perfume of magnolias, as if it had seeped into the wood paneling and patterned carpet. As if the goodness of the past could overcome the violence of the present.

But I knew better.

I found them in the salon. No swanky parties greeted me. Just my brother, sitting at one of the tables, flanked by two more sentinels.

His right eye looked puffy already, and I had no doubt it would ring with brown. His lip had a red slit down the side. A bruise was forming on his jaw. A sound escaped me, one of sympathy and horror and frustration.

Benny looked up, a hopeful expression twisting his swollen face. "Grace! I thought you weren't coming."

I went to him, ignoring the two men surrounding him. At least they didn't try to stop me when I ran my hands over my older brother's shoulders—lightly, checking him, assuring myself that he was alive.

"Of course I came," I whispered urgently. "But you know I don't have that much money."

I had been working a twelve-hour shift, so I'd found the note when I got home. *I'm in trouble, sis. Big trouble. I need to borrow $5K. Bring it to the magnolia.* Five thousand dollars? He had gotten in deeper than I suspected. Five thousand dollars, thrown away on slot machines and ceramic chips.

Five thousand dollars that I definitely didn't have. I had about half that saved up, which had all come from my art sales. Since I'd only made sales thanks to Benny—and since he was my brother—I had brought that money with me.

"Well, well. The cavalry has arrived."

God, that voice. That low, teasing voice used to turn my insides to liquid. Honestly it still did, but I knew better than to believe in it.

The sleeves of his dress shirt had been rolled up. His slacks alternately draped and hugged his long legs in all the right places. He was a handsome picture, purely male and tailored power.

And I hated him.

I tried to channel all that hate into a single word. His name. So familiar and yet completely foreign to me now. "Liam."

Whatever effect I'd been going for, it wasn't that half smile. A quirk of his lips. A sparkle in his eye. I hated how happy he could be in this moment, when he'd just assaulted my brother. Or ordered someone to do it, more likely.

In that moment I wanted to hit back. "I despise you. You are a horrible human being, and the Liam I knew, my friend, would have hated who you are now."

For a second, his expression flickered. Was that remorse? But then a cool mask slid into place. "Aren't you glad I turned you down, then, all those years ago."

He didn't say it like a question. Which was a good thing, because I hadn't been glad. The fourteen-year-old version of me had been devastated when I'd asked him to be my boyfriend. He'd been too old for me, eighteen by then, but I hadn't understood that. He'd let me down gently, so gently, saying he had to focus on his work now, focus on making something of himself—but he'd wait for me. That's what he said. He'd wait for me to grow up.

And I had believed him, but I hadn't known that his work was loan sharking and whatever other illegal enterprises he had. I hadn't known that making something of himself meant turning into a criminal. It had been five years since that day, and though I mostly pretended it had never happened, sometimes a deep feeling of humiliation would heat me from the inside out.

Like it did now, raising the temperature of my whole body and making my cheeks burn. I fumbled through my purse. "Here. I don't have the whole amount. I have two thousand."

He stared at the slim wad of bills in my outstretched hand with an expression of distaste.

I pushed it toward him. "Just take it. I'll get the rest to you, somehow. I swear. Just let my brother go."

"You only have two thousand dollars," he repeated slowly.

Did he not believe me? "It's everything I have. I cleaned out my account. I didn't even keep any back for rent, but my paycheck comes in a week and…I'll figure something out."

He looked at me oddly. "Where's the rest of your money?"

Was he trying to humiliate me? "I don't have any other money. Just what I make at the nursing home. It barely covers my bills. The only reason I have this much is from the paintings my brother sold."

At that Liam looked at my brother, and I felt Benny stiffen in his seat. Some silent conversation was taking place that I couldn't understand.

"What is it?" I asked, afraid to know the truth. This whole business was dirty—and terrifying.

"Your precious brother, the one you rushed here to save, has been stealing from you."

"What? No."

"Go ahead. Ask him."

The thing that convinced me was Liam's almost sympathetic expression. I turned to Benny with a sick feeling in my stomach. "Benny?" When he didn't answer—didn't even look at me—I asked again, with a faint note of hysteria this time. "Bennett?"

"I sold them for more than I told you," he mumbled.

I stared at him, uncomprehending. I didn't want to comprehend that my own brother had lied to me. *Stolen from me.*

My paintings had been a hobby. A passion, but something I did on the side, in private. My brother had convinced me to start selling them—I'd thought he was being supportive! But I hadn't known where to sell them. Working extra shifts at the nursing home, I hadn't had time to figure it out, either. But Benny had known. He'd sold five of my paintings in the last two months, for four hundred dollars apiece.

It was only fair that he'd taken a percentage as

commission. I'd insisted on that.

"How much did you sell them for?" I asked in a small voice.

"A thousand each," he mumbled through puffy, split lips. "Then two thousand on the last one, 'cause it was bigger."

Jesus. He'd kept so much money from me. My own brother had done that.

"He stole from me too, in a way." Liam's words were seductive, promising me absolution for my anger at my brother. "He borrowed money and promised to give it back. Except he didn't. That's why he's here. You know that. Because he's a liar and a thief."

My throat felt thick. "You tricked him. He has a problem. An addiction. The gambling—"

"Excuses. Didn't you check him into that clinic six months ago? That cost you a pretty penny. And what did he do?"

He'd checked himself right back out, wasting the three-thousand-dollar enrollment fee. It had been money painstakingly saved up from the whole time I'd worked as a custodian at the nursing home. Then when I'd graduated high school, I'd been promoted to an orderly. I had thought maybe one day I could save enough for nursing school…but God, that would never happen. I had been crazy to think it would. There was barely anything left over in my paycheck after bills and food. And anytime I did save money, Benny's addiction ate it up.

Benny hung his head, unable or unwilling to defend himself.

I was suddenly feeling far less sympathetic about his injuries. In truth, I had shown up expecting it to be worse. I'd had terrible visions of broken bones and severed fingers. But maybe I'd been overreacting. Maybe Liam still had that spark of humanity, of compassion, I'd once loved as a child. And even if I knew Benny was partly to blame for his situation, I couldn't leave him to the wolves. Namely, one wolf. Liam.

I turned to my childhood friend who looked so different now with the glint of scruff on his face, with a bend in his nose where it had been broken. He looked so much more distinguished. He looked intimidating.

"Please let him go. Even if he… I know what he did. But he's my brother. I can't leave here without him. Take the two thousand. I'll get you more, soon. I promise you. Just don't hurt him."

"Do you know how much he owes me, Grace?"

I swallowed. "Five thousand dollars?"

His face pulled into a slight grimace. He sighed. "Fifteen."

I stood there, stunned. Unable to gasp or even breathe. Fifteen thousand dollars. I would never have that much money, not ever. But he was *my brother*.

"Please," I whispered, reduced to begging.

Liam looked away, and for a horrible second I thought it was a refusal. My stomach pitched wildly, in fear and doubt and desperation. How could I fix this? I couldn't, I couldn't. My brother was going to be beaten or killed.

Then he turned back to me, a hard glint in his gunmetal eyes. "There is a way you can help. You can be mine, Grace. Mine to do whatever I want with."

Seconds passed with excruciating slowness as my mind protected me. Then reality slammed into me—all at once. He meant sex. I was almost sure he meant sex. Then I laughed at myself, hollow and jaded. What else would it mean?

I hadn't thought it possible to hate Liam more, but I did, because he'd set up an impossible choice. For fifteen thousand dollars—and for my brother's safety—I had to agree.

What did that make me? A prostitute? A sex slave?

An expensive one, at least.

I looked at my brother as the offer stood in the air. He wouldn't meet my eyes. Couldn't he at least put up a token protest? At least *try* to protect my honor? But I was getting a clearer picture of Benny than I had our whole lives. Letting himself fall to this level was one thing, but dragging me into it was the last straw. I would do this for him—and that was it.

"Never again," I whispered.

I would never drain my bank account and come running to help ever again. Never sell my body for him. Never trust my brother again. It was like losing a family member. The only one I had.

Benny nodded, or maybe he was just drifting out of

consciousness, his head bobbing slightly. Who knew? I was done. I would do what Liam required of me, and then I would be finished. Finished with family. Finished with criminals.

I'd be alone then.

I nodded grimly. "I'll do it."

Liam gestured to his goons. "Show him out." Then he turned back to me with a guarded look. What was he protecting himself against? "This way."

I stared after him for a second. What had I gotten myself into? But it was too late to back out. Benny was already being strong-armed out the door. Well, if I was honest, he wasn't being forced at all. He was practically running out the door, and he didn't look back. He wasn't a fool.

I was the fool.

My heart beat an erratic pattern. If I tried to bolt, would his men stop me? Would Liam himself restrain me if I fought him? He'd purchased the right to use me, in a way. That didn't mean I'd make it easy.

He led me down the hallway I'd come from, and into a more expansive lobby. A massive chandelier filled the domed ceiling. Some long-gone centerpiece had left a patch of vibrant-colored carpet in the middle of the room. Why had he picked this place for his headquarters? Even in its decay, it was too beautiful for cruelty.

A mechanical groan sounded from behind the elevator doors, then a crash as the steel box settled on its ancient cables. Liam opened the gold crisscross gate and gestured me inside. When I stayed rooted to the spot, he said impatiently, "I've had the building inspected. It's perfectly safe."

As if *that* was why I'd hesitate to step inside.

But I had no other options. Even if he let me leave now, there was no way to get fifteen thousand dollars. And deep down, I didn't want to leave the Magnolia Hotel, the place I'd made elaborate fantasies about all my life, and go back to my one-room apartment with the bass pounding through the walls. The hotel had seemed like a castle, a place both pretty and safe. And now inhabited by a dragon.

"Coming?" the dragon asked.

I stepped inside.

✧　✧　✧

THE ELEVATORS HAD never been working when I played here as a kid. And the stairwells chained shut. But now the rattling motor took us up. And up and up. To the penthouse, the very top. A mishmashed version of me looked back at me through the milky-white reflective mirrors. Then the elevator doors opened, and I was looking at a Magnolia Hotel room. An actual room, and it was so much better than I could have imagined.

The sofas had elaborate silhouettes carved into dark wood. The fabric upholstery was floral and damask and a strange satiny substance that reflected light from crystal-dripped lamps. Like the carpet downstairs, there were bright rectangles left in the wallpaper from where pictures would have hung.

Ruthlessly, I tamped down my pleasure. This wasn't about sightseeing, even if I *was* finally seeing the sight of my dreams. This was about obligation and pain. It was about the man who stood watching me a few feet away with hooded eyes and a slightly resentful turn of his lips. For someone about to get his way, he didn't seem very happy. Maybe he didn't really want me. Maybe he was reconsidering.

"Will you change your mind?" I asked.

A flicker of surprise. "Never."

That couldn't be relief I felt.

"Would you like a drink?" A brass cart held an array of amber liquids and cut-glass decanters.

"Please. Yes."

He poured me something that went down smooth as silk. I drank the whole glass and then felt slightly dizzy.

"Slow down," he said.

Easy for him to say. He didn't have to look forward to a whole night of…what, exactly? I didn't know what would happen next, or how it would happen, or how many times it would happen. My nerves were jittery, nonstop and overbright, like a neon sign flickering in an old pawn shop. He was so solicitous now, so patient all of a sudden. Everything felt too slow, as if time itself had slammed on the breaks. I wanted this over and done with. I wanted to never do it at all.

"Are you going to be rough?" I whispered.

"Do you want me to?"

"Yes," I said, because then I could really hate him. And I'd know for sure, for absolute sure, that we had never been meant to be. That wasn't how I liked sex. *This* wasn't how I liked sex, forced and dispassionate. I would never like sex with Liam.

Oh God, I couldn't do this. I imagined him twisting my arm and pushing me into the ground. I imagined his face contorting in anger and disgust. I had buried the feelings for him long ago, but every unkind word or cold touch would dig them up. And then where would I be? Devastated, like I was when I heard what he'd become. He'd be using not only my body but my childish love for him, my lingering hope. He'd use all of me for his own pleasure and then send me home, disheveled and hollow.

The empty glass rolled from my nerveless fingers, soundless on the carpet pile. I bolted for the door, also soundless. Also empty. It was a frantic flight, like a bird bursting from a bush, except I couldn't actually fly. And I had already been locked inside a cage. I reached the elevator doors at the same second as he caught me from behind. He spun me around, and there was the anger I had dreaded to see. Anger and disgust.

"You'd break your promise? That's not the Grace I knew."

I laughed. "I guess people change when they get older."

"Yeah," he muttered. "They do."

As if to prove his point, he turned me with my wrist, twisting my arm until I faced the wall. Faded wallpaper against my cheek. A hard body pinning me from behind. Trapped. Trapped in the prettiest cage. A tear slipped down my cheek.

He made a sound of annoyance. "Am I as horrible as that? To let me touch you? Are my hands that dirty?"

"You hit my brother!"

"You're right, I did. He stole from me. And unlike you, I'm not going to be a martyr. I take what's mine."

He reached around my body. His hands were rough on my breasts, mauling me, hurting me—on purpose. Spoken insults would not be enough for him. He had to show me, with a hard grip on soft flesh and a cruel pinch of my nipple. I cried out, and he grew slightly more gentle, but his hands still roamed me with utter possession. They roamed over my hips and low over my belly to the space between my legs.

"How do you like it?" His breath was hot against my temple. "Not rough, I know that. Do you like it soft and slow, with music playing in the background? Should I have hired a violinist to seduce you first?"

He was mocking me. I jerked in his arms, but he subdued me quickly—with just a single finger. He reached under my skirt, and when his forefinger slipped beneath the hem of my panties, I froze. He moved lower until he brushed the private hair there.

Then he froze too.

We waited like that, while he touched such a private

place. Just touched, nothing more. It had become a Rubicon—that coarse, trimmed hair. Any farther and there would be no turning back. We both knew it. But that was the thing about rivers; they couldn't control when they were crossed.

"Say yes, Grace."

"Do I have a choice?"

His voice turned gravelly, his breath erratic. "Say yes."

I didn't really have a choice, because it wasn't only about this moment with him and me. It was about my brother and our childhood. It was about all the circumstances that had led to this. Maybe it was inevitable that he and I would be together. Maybe everything had been leading to this.

"Yes."

He took me at my word, dipping low to the damp lips of my sex. I shivered with the sudden touch, but just as quickly, it was gone. He spun me around and pressed me back into the wall.

His mouth fused to mine, a sudden onslaught I should have been prepared for but wasn't. I gasped, and that gave him the opening he needed. He pushed inside, all tongue and teeth and a need I couldn't have predicted. He touched every part of my mouth, reaching inside, hungry for it. For me.

I stood there, passive, in a state of shock. I couldn't comprehend all the ways he could touch me. Hot and wet with his mouth. Firm and controlling with his hands. His whole body was flush against mine, pulsing with his arousal. I could feel his erection against my belly, could feel his excitement in the pant of his breath. And deep inside, I felt him too.

My body stirred, preparing itself for him. That's all this was, a clinical procedure. He would be inserting, and I would receive him. Lube was required for such an act, and so my body produced it, slickening my folds and throbbing with readiness.

Except nothing about this felt clinical, not the old-world penthouse or the man almost rabid with need. Nothing about this felt real, and I let the magical pretend quality float me away.

This was a dream. A thing that wasn't really happening.

I could enjoy it.

"Kiss me back," he muttered as his lips moved over my jaw.

The first touch of my hand on his chest, tentative, made him groan low in his throat. I curled my fingers around his collar and tugged gently. He pushed hard against me—no finesse, just shoved me straight into the wall with his body, as if he could join us that way. Not with his cock or his tongue, just pressing so hard that we'd be one person.

When his lips met mine again, I opened for him. I let him inside and did more than that. I touched my tongue against his. I was trembling. A leaf on the sidewalk, moving with the wind. He should crush me with that kind of force, but all I did was flit and tumble, turning over and over, dizzy with passion.

I woke up though, a little, when he pulled away. It was impossible to remain completely dazed when he looked at me that way. My shirt was pulled up, revealing my breasts. My skirt was around my waist—the work his hands had done. I was exposed for him, but he didn't look at my body.

He looked me straight in the eyes when he said, "I've wanted you for so long."

Then it felt all too real, and I didn't know what to do with that. I didn't know where to put these feelings inside me except in the bins marked *wrong* and *gullible* and *stupid little girl.* I wasn't a girl anymore. I shouldn't want him at all.

I couldn't stand the way he looked at me. As if I wasn't a child, and not just because I could have sex now. But because he wanted something deeper from me, something more meaningful than a girlish crush. Except I had nothing left to give him.

Desperate to direct his attention away, I asked, "Where's the bedroom?"

Disappointment flickered in his eyes, so briefly I might not have seen it. Might not have recognized it, if I hadn't felt the same thing five years ago when he'd told me no, he wouldn't be my boyfriend.

He said he'd wait for me.

But it had been a long time since I believed a word he said. He may not have meant that promise to a teenaged girl, but I could only hope he followed through on this deal with Benny's debt. I had sold him my body but not my heart. He could use one all he wanted. I wouldn't let him touch the other.

THE BED WAS a bad idea. It had been my idea, so I couldn't even pin this on Liam. I could pin the whole blackmail-coercion-sex on him, sure, but the bed had been my lame attempt at distraction, and here we were.

Beds were for lovers. They were for staying up late talking and sleeping in. They were for passionate sex with someone you actually cared about. We weren't going to do any of that. He was going to use me, and I was going to be used. That was the point, really. The coercion had to be part of the appeal for him, because he was a handsome man. Objectively I admitted he could get any woman he wanted. So the only reason he'd done this was to make me feel like shit.

And it was working. I sat in the middle of the bed, my clothes rumpled and twisted around me, miserable. I thought about running again, but it was more of a hypothetical than an actual plan. He would only catch me again. And where would I go? The word *home* was a joke. My cold apartment was just a room. I felt more at home in the courtyard of the Magnolia than I ever had in the trailer park I'd grown up in.

He wandered to the corner of the room, and I could almost believe he was detached, if he hadn't been practically inhaling me sixty seconds ago. The tension in the room was electric, raising the hair on my arms and shooting sparks through my body.

"Undress for me."

I knew the way he meant it. Not just taking off my clothes to give him access. He meant a striptease, but I had no idea how to put on a sexy show. I'd only had sex with one guy, a boyfriend in my senior year of high school, and both of us had fumbled our way through the dark.

It had been awkward but also intimate. Raw. That was me—unpolished. If Liam had wanted a stripper, why hadn't he hired an actual professional who knew what she was doing?

Because he wanted to humiliate me.

That was the only answer. And I resented him for it, even though I knew it wasn't quite fair. After all, he was basically paying $15,000 for the dubious privilege. The deal helped me more than it did him, so I should really stop hating him—but I couldn't.

My first moves were jerky and uncoordinated. My shirt came off in bits—one arm and then these leftover buttons and then this other arm. The skirt didn't fare much better. I had to unbunch it from my waist and smooth it out before it could come down. And then my panties, which were serviceable white. My bra was last, which seemed backward, really. And he'd already seen my breasts earlier, when he pushed the white lace aside. But still I blushed when the straps fell down my arms. I held the cups to my chest, hoping.

He approached me like a panther, low to the ground, but that was an illusion. He had power, so much power. The power to pinch the center of my bra, the ribbon connecting to the two sides, between his forefinger and thumb. He tugged, so gently, and I had to let it go. Had to let go of modesty and pride and hope as it landed with a quiet *whoosh*.

Finally, finally, I met his eyes. It didn't matter that what I'd done was awkward and ungainly, his eyes still burned with a kind of want I couldn't quite comprehend. What would it feel like to want someone's body quite that much, as if it were air and water and land—as if the person were earth itself and home besides?

"Will you hate me after this?" he asked mildly, as if he didn't care about the answer. I suspected he did care, though. I suspected that some part of that laughing, teasing boy was still inside, the one who would never have made me cry.

Until he did.

"I already hate you," I answered softly.

"Then this won't matter."

And then he was pushing me, laying me back onto the bed. He didn't kiss me this time—not on the mouth. He nuzzled my breasts, kissing me there instead. He nibbled his way down the curve of them as if taking their measure. His mouth closed around my breast, hot and teasing. The suction pushed my hips off the bed, pressing against his body, futile and rhythmic.

He pushed my hips back down. "Stay."

Stay down, he meant. Stay still. Not seeking my own pleasure. My cheeks heated with embarrassment. When had I started to enjoy this? I *couldn't* enjoy this. But I couldn't deny the throb in my pussy either. It clenched and clenched, wanting to be filled.

He wouldn't though. Maybe he was a sadist after all, because he knew exactly what my body wanted and he refused, moving down my hip instead. He kissed the curve of my hip, and then he—he bit me. Right there, where the skin smoothed over muscle and bone. Where it hurt. I yelped, just a little, and then his tongue was on me, soothing over the spot.

His gaze met mine as he slid a hand between my legs.

I tensed, even though it was too late for doubts or second chances. He didn't give me time anyway. He just found my slit with an accuracy that unnerved me. He pushed two fingers inside—it wasn't even dry. No, the slippery channel accepted his fingers readily, just sucked them in, greedy. I couldn't do anything but lie there, feeling my body betray me.

Then it got worse.

He lowered his head and…licked my clit. Just licked it with the flat of his tongue, and the pleasure was sharp enough to be pain. My legs trembled with the effort to stay open. I wanted to snap them shut, to keep him out. But he was already there, already with his fingers inside me and his lips circling my clit. He sucked, and I had to disobey—my hips came off the bed. He'd told me not to, he'd told me to stay as if I were dog, but I couldn't listen to him anyway. Pure need coursed through my clit, my pussy. It throbbed in my breasts, even when he reached up and caressed them.

I couldn't understand why he was doing this instead of hurting me. Instead of humiliating me.

God, that tongue. It felt like silk, like he was wrapping all around me from that one small place. Like he was binding me and no matter how hard I bucked and pushed with my hips, I couldn't break free. I only wanted more, and his fingers—thank the Lord for those fingers—they searched inside me, finding the key. He twisted his hand, just so, and then I broke apart, coming on his fingers and against his mouth, crying out his name as if he would save me.

My body still pulsed when he withdrew. His lips glistened with my arousal.

He could have mocked me for this. I'd said I hated him and then came for him harder than I'd ever come. It could have been his crowning moment, except he didn't look mocking or cruel. Instead he looked…desperate. His cheeks were flushed with color, his breath coming in bellows. When he stood up, I could see the erection tenting his pants, almost completely horizontal despite the wool fabric restraining it. He looked close to bursting, and unbidden, a sense of tenderness rose up in me.

I sat up and reached for his belt. He let me unbuckle

and unzip him while he dealt with his shirt. I pulled down his boxers too, and he hissed in a breath as the air met his erection. I could understand why, when I saw how hard he was, how red and taut the skin was. He must be sensitive there. So sensitive it would ache, and I understood that.

I thought I would return the favor and suck him, but he pushed me back so I was lying on the bed. He climbed up, straddling my torso, holding his cock in his fist.

"I'm sorry," he said hoarsely. "If this is the only time I get with you, I have to do this now."

Do what now? I wasn't sure, but I got the idea when he fondled my breasts. When he pulled the nipples until they were hard and red points. When he stroked himself roughly and quickly, then I knew.

He wanted to come on my breasts.

That was his fantasy, the one he had to do now, his only chance. It made me feel strange inside, part aroused and part proud, like I had done this to him. Like I'd meant something, even if it was only a tawdry sexual dream.

But oh, when he came, it didn't feel tawdry at all. His face screwed up into a mask of agony and ecstasy. His fist jerked once, twice, pulling back to expose the shiny head of his cock. It jetted out creamy streams onto my breasts, my belly, hot and shocking.

He painted me that way, the way I painted a canvas—honest and vulnerable. And even though I should hate him for this, should probably feel low about what had just happened, I stroked his thigh, soothing, telling him without words that this part, at least, had been safe.

✧ ✧ ✧

HE GOT A warm washcloth and cleaned me up, but I could see sleep overtaking him. I could see the shadows under his eyes. From stress? Why wasn't he sleeping? And why did I care? Then it didn't matter anymore, because he climbed into the bed and pulled me close.

A few minutes later, the steady rhythm of his breath told me he was sleeping.

With his arms circling me and his leg flung over me and his face pressed into my hair, he was sleeping. It made my heart feel full, and I couldn't deny what it meant anymore. I wasn't falling for him; I was already at the lowest point. I'd fallen in love with him as a teenager, and no amount of denial or anger or wishing things different had changed that.

And it was useless. He had just, essentially, paid me to have sex with him. It had been a form of coercion, really, with the threat to my brother in the same room. That wasn't the basis for a relationship. Even if he wanted one.

Even if *I* wanted one.

God, this was crazy. It made me shake and twist in my own skin, as if I couldn't figure myself out. And it was too hot, far too hot in the embrace of his body. I had to pull away, to catch my breath.

But when I stood up, naked in the dark hotel room, I wasn't sure where to go next. I could get dressed and leave. I wasn't sure if the guards at the doors would stop me, but I could try a fire escape. But what if Liam got mad and thought I'd reneged on the deal? What if he went after Benny again?

Except…what had he said at the end? He'd said if this was the only time he had with me. As if we might not have sex again. And I didn't understand how that would work when I owed him fifteen thousand dollars, when we'd made this deal to compensate him. How could one time be worth fifteen thousand dollars?

Maybe the sex was only interest, designed to delay the full payment. I really should have made him spell out the details when we'd made the deal. But I'd never been a good businessperson, which was why Benny had sold my paintings for me—even though that hadn't turned out well either.

I found his dress shirt crumpled on the floor. When I pulled it on, the musky scent of him suffused me. I wandered into the living room again, running my fingertip along the wall.

Whatever illegal things had been done in this room since Liam had bought the place, they hadn't changed the building itself. It still vibrated with a sort of charm and goodwill. It still made me feel safe.

Did he live up here, in the penthouse? He must, because although the room was clean, I saw a book propped like a tent on a side table and a half-empty coffee mug on the small dining table. That meant he also slept in the bed where we'd just had sex.

He'd sleep there again tonight. But would I?

I felt a little like a voyeur walking through his rooms. The wires in my brain had crossed. I was curious about the Magnolia Hotel; I was curious about Liam. I couldn't separate them anymore. I loved the hotel…and I couldn't pretend to hate Liam anymore. Not after what we'd just done.

The last room I came to was a study.

It had gorgeous walnut siding and a beautiful carved desk, but I couldn't think about those. All I saw were the paintings on the walls. Four of them, one for each wall. And another one propped up against the wall as if waiting to be hung.

My paintings.

Vivid royal blues and a pale peachy pink. Damask fading into a rusted copper.

My breath came short and then not at all. I clutched my hands to my stomach as if it could hold me in, rein back what I felt, what I hoped. I'd always known that the hotel inspired me, both real and imagined. But what I hadn't realized was that I'd been painting *for* the hotel. That these painting were designed to fit here and become part of the place I loved.

Liam had bought them. This was how he'd known for sure my brother was cheating me.

He had bought them for a lot of money too, and why would he do that if my family already owed him money? In fact, why would he make that deal with me, when I would have found a way to pay him the debt, when he could have had another woman for far less, for nothing at all?

A sound came from the door. He stood wearing only his slacks, leaning against the door frame but looking far from casual.

"So, you found them." His voice gave him away. Gravelly and thick with leftover sleep.

"You bought my paintings," I said, shaken.

"Yeah, well. You're a good artist. I always said that."

He had told me that. Back when we'd been kids and I'd squeezed every last drop from the tubes of paint to make them last. Later, I'd assumed he was just being nice to the little girl from the same trailer park, the one with a crush on him.

My tongue felt tied up in knots. "You said you'd wait for me."

"I said I'd wait for you to grow up. And you did."

"Then why…all this?" I waved my hand. Why the Magnolia Hotel and my brother? Why force me?

"Would you have come any other way?"

No, he was right about that. I would have slammed the door in his face, hurt about what he had turned into. Afraid of it. He still scared me, but I also knew now that he loved me.

He shrugged. "I told you. I'm not a martyr. I take what's mine."

But he wouldn't really, I knew that too. What he'd

said as he came over me, that it might be our last time, it was because he wouldn't force me to be here if I didn't want to. He wouldn't force me to come back.

There was only one problem with that. I wanted to stay.

"I won't fight you," I whispered.

He tried to hide how that affected him; he really did. He swallowed and looked away. "Grace, I know this is wrong."

I shook my head, but he didn't see. So I went up to him. I reached out and turned his chin toward me. His gaze met mine. I reached down, to that honest and vulnerable place, the same place I painted from. "This is the only thing that's ever been right in my life."

I meant him, most of all. But I also meant the Magnolia Hotel and the sex we'd had and the unholy deal we had made. They were all connected now, meshed like paint on the canvas, inseparable.

His eyes burned with emotion, spilling over. "I'm never going to let you leave."

And I took it for the promise it was. He took me again, right there in the office, making a mess on the antique desk. He made love to me there and in every single room, and I loved the Magnolia Hotel after all.

Want more from Skye Warren? You can download TOUGH LOVE, a dark mafia romance for free!

Unlawful Seduction
Pam Godwin

AT SOME POINT in Dev's forensics career, he'd landed smack in the middle of Kansas, where the people were as predictable and mundane as their crimes. And now in the hard thrust of winter, he questioned the wisdom of choosing a place where the windchill sucked his dick into his body and dried out his balls.

But Ms. Joni Torpey wasn't flying in from LA to meet with him about the weather. The ass-clenching journalist represented Flotter Film, a documentary production company. She was due for their seven PM meeting to interview him on the motivations of sex crimes, a subject in which he'd received numerous accreditations. *Detective Devon Burgess, the country's leading expert in paraphilic behavior. An authority on serial debauchery and sexual rituals.*

There was a reason he understood the blurred lines between arousal and transgression. It was the same reason he'd left his niche in New Orleans, the city of temptation. But no one knew about that. Besides, it wasn't that bad. He was still employed in detective work. He was still considered an expert. He still hadn't acted out his darkest fantasies.

The heady roast of coffee flavored the air and warmed Dev's gut. He swallowed the smoky dregs of his second cup and swung a foot over his knee. He'd chosen the chair by the fireplace for its angled view of the back counter and the front door.

The only two customers—men who were too young to spark his sexual interests—straddled old wood chairs at the bar and frowned at their handheld devices. Buttery leather couches and low-lit lamps invited extended lounging. The coffee shop was reminiscent of a rich man's den and not much larger.

The twentysomething barista fidgeted with the espresso machine. She kept her eyes down but grumbled to herself with more volume than was needed. If she wanted male attention, she should lose her eternal scowl. It was remarkable how much one could achieve with a smile alone.

The door rattled open. He shifted his focus to the glass counter filled with specialty cheeses and pastries, keeping the entrance in his periphery. Casual and unassuming, he was a man enjoying a coffee in a little hidden nook. He was not a leashed predator, scoping and waiting for something…enticing. Like an unsuspecting man or woman to follow home, with begging lips to gag and a tight body to paint with his come.

His cock twitched against the seam of his slacks, but his desires were internal, stalking him and him alone.

A gust of frigid air bustled in with the shuffle of

heels. In a tangle of long blonde hair, a woman skidded to a stop in the entryway. She rubbed her hands together, staring at them with a shell-shocked look on her face. Then she glanced up at the barista and the two men at the bar, and blinked rapidly. "I'm not from around here, but seriously, it's as cold as…" She sniffed. "Okay, nothing's that cold. I just lost my friginity out there."

And just like that, grins sprouted through the room, cracking every expression, including his.

She huffed a drawn-out exhale over her pink fingers. "I'll take the hottest drink you got, with a double shot of scalding." The profile of her pink lips bowed up, rounding her flushed cheeks.

Mother of God, her smile leaped the space between them, curled its warmth around him and settled in a low burn between his legs. If she was the journalist, her carefree demeanor and natural glow went well beyond the polished-blonde look so common in TV personalities. Maybe Ms. Joni Torpey wasn't an ass clencher after all.

She wove toward the counter, teeth chattering, shoulders bunched.

"House coffee to go, ma'am?" The barista still wore her grin.

"For here, thanks." She leaned a hip on the counter, her body angled toward him and the men at the bar, but her attention clung to the display of pastries. "And some of that yummy brown bread."

Her curve-hugging dress exposed golden skin from her midthighs to her ankle boots. The cropped length of her unzipped leather jacket catered to LA couture, not Midwest winters. No wonder she was freezing her tits off.

The douches at the bar seemed to have forgotten their devices in lieu of ogling her erect nipples. Fuck, he was staring too.

"I'll bring your order to you." The barista waved a hand over the room. "Go warm up."

"Lovely. Thank you." All four corners of the shop offered seating, but she turned unerringly toward his.

Their eyes locked, and his breath hitched. The graceful rise of her cheekbones caught the dim light, illuminating her fresh-faced complexion and dainty features. The puckered lift of her lips, her tiny upright nose, and the arch of one narrow eyebrow cast an expression glimmering with amusement.

He wanted to see that look while her naked body was strung up and spread open, his dick thrusting into each and every hole.

Blood rushed below his belt. If he didn't rein it in, he wouldn't be able to stand without revealing the nature of his thoughts. Not that he had a problem with public arousal.

She slid one long leg in front of the other and closed the distance. He knew he was smiling like an asshole, but his cheeks refused to relax, so he gave her a chin lift.

Her eyes didn't sway from his as he adjusted himself

and stood. A coffee table separated the two chairs in his little corner, and he suddenly wished he'd chosen the spot over there, the one with the single love seat they could share. So he could smell her. And accidentally touch her. Because he was a fucking pervert.

And not the only one. The men at the bar watched with gaping jaws as she glided past them, her strides as easygoing as the lift of her mouth. The temperature of the room stoked to blazing. He tugged at his collar. Was there a law against a fetish for beautiful smiles? Smilephilia? He'd found a new kink to poke at the hundred trapped ones in his head.

He shifted around the table and came face-to-face with sparkling hazel eyes.

"You must be Detective Devon Burgess. I'm Joni Torpey." With an outstretched hand, she grinned up at him, her mouth curling in gentle peaks.

He clasped her hand, his fingers enclosing icicles. "Gloves are advisable in single-digit temperatures."

She tightened her grip. "Good to know for the next time I never come here again."

Smart-ass. "Call me Dev, and you've got me till closing time." He glanced at his watch. "Which is at—"

"Nine o'clock. We've got two hours." She released his hand and adjusted the briefcase strap on her shoulder. "Thank you so much for agreeing to the interview."

To think he'd almost declined it. The only specs his background check had turned up was her clean criminal,

DMV, and tax history, and her birth records. She'd just turned thirty-four. Five years his junior. "We could've done this over Skype."

"Nope." She shook her head, silky blonde hair swishing around her face. "This is more effective. The energy transmitted in body language and expressions is as valuable as verbal responses."

No dispute there. Her vividness was a stark contrast from her stoic e-mail. "You're not like the journalists who usually interview me." When her eyebrows lifted, he said, "Are you going to clench your ass every time I mention the word *sex*?"

Her tongue tapped her front teeth. "Will you need to perform an anal cavity search to check for clenching?"

A whiplash of lust quickened his breath. She might as well have cupped him and squeezed. *Get a grip, dickhead.* She was teasing, not begging for a cock in her ass. "Only if you require one, Ms. Torpey." He smirked.

"Joni." She returned his smirk.

"Have a seat, Joni." He gestured toward the one he'd vacated beside the fireplace.

When she settled, her head cocked, teeth sawing the plump flesh of her bottom lip. Her soft gaze traced his mouth and wandered down his chest as he took the seat opposite hers. She wasn't even trying to hide her interest. His desperate mind whispered possibilities, and all of the scenarios included a night that extended beyond two hours.

He cleared his throat. "When did you fly in?"

"Just arrived. I fly back in the morning."

His chest caved in, sinking his hope for a long weekend between her legs. "Where are you staying?"

"In town."

Watching her enticing lips form that wisely vague answer, he felt like a hunter. Hungry. Calculating. And usually a hell of a lot more subtle. He leaned back in a display of carefree and nowhere to be. "Fire when ready, Joni."

"All right." She removed a laptop from her bag and powered it on. "As I mentioned in my e-mail, our researchers are interviewing a selection of psychiatrists, law enforcement, and felons." She shrugged. "I got the paraphilia expert."

For as long as she wanted him. Hopefully, her interest lasted till morning. He nodded.

The barista arrived with the bread and coffee and returned to the counter.

Joni sipped from her cup, rolling back her shoulders and smiling. Then she set it aside and met his eyes. "The documentary examines arousal in its myriad of scents. Our mission is to isolate the poisoned, disease-ridden odors, and air out why only certain people are corrupted by them."

Cute. Did she rehearse that? Maybe it was a quote from the film. "Everyone has unsavory fantasies. You want to know what rouses a person to act on them?"

With the keyboard balanced on her lap, she nodded. "Is it power and control, anger, or some mental disorder?"

"Or horniness."

She blinked. "Everyone gets horny, Detective—"

"Dev." He wanted to taste her responses without the stiffness of job titles.

"Fine, Dev. What takes a person from horny to unlawful?"

Rather than tire them both with a didactic monologue, he decided to answer with a little harmless flirting. "A guy stands behind you in a checkout line, watching your ass as you bend over to retrieve something from beneath your cart. When you stand up, he brushes his erection against your backside. You may or may not feel it."

A smile danced in her eyes. "Frotteurism."

"Horny. What about the guy who randomly dials your number late at night and whispers all the ways he wants to fuck you, his breath heavy, his voice so compelling you find you're unable to hang up."

"Phone scatologia is stalking and harassment." She glanced up, and her pupils dilated. "And I would hang up." Her hand went to her hoop earring, rubbing a finger over the hook. Then she released it to lift her coffee cup. More likely, she realized stroking her jewelry was an indication of her arousal.

He leaned his elbows on his thighs and captured her gaze. "You sure you'd hang up?"

Her knees pinched together, the nonverbal answer heating the air. If he called her from an unknown number, he would murmur his illicit fantasies and fuck his hand to the sound of her gasps. A warm flush coursed through his body.

"Making vulgar phone calls is a disorder." She blew out a breath. "And a Class 1 Misdemeanor."

Only in some states. "Since we're discussing hypothetical scenarios, what if I jerked off right here, while you watched? How would you label that?"

Caught in the sharpest stare he had, she didn't flinch. "Exhibitionism. You would be arrested."

"Or horniness. That shouldn't be a crime."

A lovely red hue tinted her cheeks, from the warmth of the coffee, the nearby fire and her arousal. "So you believe the motivation is mere horniness, not mental conditions or power plays?"

The front door slammed, and a glance over his shoulder revealed empty bar stools. The barista's footsteps shuffled in the back room. They were alone. He turned back to her.

"Tell me about the opposite end of the spectrum." Her fingers hovered over the keyboard.

Either she found his directness uncomfortable, or she truly wanted to understand criminal sexuality. His chest collapsed. Any sexual interest he might've kindled in her was about to be extinguished, but he was there to answer her questions. "You mean rape, pedophilia and sexual murder?"

At her nod, he sifted through his recollection of the worst kinds of criminals. For the next hour, he outlined their profiles, methods, degrees of force, and typologies. She clicked on her keys as he spoke, her shoulders deflating and her jaw sliding back and forth. He'd shredded a napkin on the table between them, suffocating in the miasma of putrid subject matter.

When he finished his walk-through on human depravity, she leaned back and shook out her hands. "And the motivation?"

"Pursuit of sadistic pleasure, power and control."

She nodded, a cloud of thoughts churning in her wide eyes. "Reeks of paraphilic disorders."

"When the victim isn't a willing adult, yes. There are erotic attractions to fear, blood, asphyxiation, children, pain, tears, bondage—"

The fluctuation in her breath jumped on the last word. Her thighs flexed together.

Oh, Joni was a naughty girl. "You want to discuss bondage?"

Her response was dismissed with her laptop as she set it on the table to unwrap the honey-wheat bread. She tore off a piece soaked with butter and slid it past her lips. "Want some?"

He shook his head, mesmerized by the movement of her mouth as she chewed. She licked her fingers, tongue curling, sucking each slender digit, the damned tease.

His breath staggered away from him as he hovered on the edge of the chair. Fuck it. He jumped to his feet and nudged the table aside with his foot. She paused midlick, watching him. He leaned down, hands on the armrests of her chair, his face a breath from hers.

They shared an impenetrable moment of eye contact, her soft expression at odds with the heave of her chest. When her hand lowered from her mouth, he caught her wrist, his fantasies shoving their way into reality. His heart hammered.

"What are you doing?" Her husky voice surged heat through his veins.

Slowly, vigilantly, he clenched the tiny bones in her arm and raised her fingers to his lips. Her breath caught, eyes smoldering, her arm pliant in his grip. Fucking perfect. Fear was not his kink.

The first touch of her fingers on his lips sent a shiver through him. She watched his mouth, unblinking, a swell of want deepening the yellow-green expanse of her irises.

He nipped at her index finger and drew it into his mouth in one long suck. The sweet and salty flavor of her skin and the breathless tremble through her body propelled him to the next finger, and the next.

Her eyelids drooped, and her mouth parted. All the right signals. He grabbed her other wrist and hoisted her to her tiptoes. With her chest pressed against his, he crossed her arms behind her back. Still no struggling and her eyes sharpened with interest.

"I think bondage is your thing, Joni." His pulse raced at the thought. He bent his head and opened her lips with his, sweeping his tongue in, coaxing hers.

She stiffened in his hold, and for a distressing moment, he was certain she would reject him. Then she fell against his mouth, sucking and licking, hands tugging against the shackle of his. He released her arms, and she plunged fingers through his hair, pulling his face closer.

He molded her slender waist against him, one hand on her jaw, the other clenching on her hip. The friction of her pelvis rubbing against his, the intense slide of her tongue chasing and tangling wrangled a moan from his throat. It was a hard, crushing grind of lips and bodies as they kissed and bit.

"We're closing in ten minutes." The fucking barista shouted from the back room.

Joni pushed against his chest, slipped from his arms, and swiped a hand over her mouth. Her breath rushed from her lungs noisily, her eyes wide and uncertain.

Goddamn it. His stomach sank.

"That wasn't supposed to happen." She sidestepped around him and crouched to slide her laptop into her bag.

The curvature of her waist and the round bend of her ass kept his arousal heated on a roiling simmer. He needed to keep the conversation going and look for an opening to extend the night. "We haven't discussed the gray areas."

She stood, her swollen lips conflicting with her narrow-eyed glare. "Do these gray areas have anything to do with that kiss?"

Why would she ask that? She didn't know the depth of his intentions. "The trickiest crimes teeter on the razored edge between seduction and coercion." The words warmed his throat, voiced from the dangerous snare of his thoughts. "We both wanted that kiss. And more." He took a step toward her. "Come home with me."

She backed up, little lines grooving her forehead.

Fuck. "I meant..." Exactly what he'd said. His throat dried. "Let's go somewhere, so we can finish the conversation for your research."

"I have what I need, Detective Burgess. I need to use the restroom. I'll see myself out. Thanks for your time."

Dismissed. No handshake. No smile. She paced away, her ass flexing with each graceful step. Motherfuck. What had scared her off? The barista? Fear of her desires, or his? He scrubbed a hand over his face, muscles contracting, ready to chase her.

Across the room, she disappeared behind the bathroom door. He moved to follow her, and his foot tangled in the strap of her laptop case. He reached down and gripped the flap, opening it. Right there in an inner pocket waited a white key-card envelope. The name of the hotel and her room number would be printed on it. If there were two key cards...

He groaned at the wretched level of his desperation. He needed to let her go. For a guy who always let them go, it shouldn't be a problem. Yet, every cell in his body fired in objection.

Frustrated and clouded with desire, he stood in his lonely corner of the coffee shop and deliberated the risks. Laws would be broken. She could have him arrested.

She could offer him her body.

He plucked out the envelope. *Blitz Luxury Suites. Room #106.* Two magnetic keys. His blood thrummed in a turbulent mess of excitement, panic and determination. He pocketed a key, counting on her to have overlooked the extra, and returned the envelope.

Never had he expected to find someone who could entice him enough to set his fantasies in motion. What if his untested seduction failed? It could cost him his job, his freedom and her trust. He gave the bathroom door a hesitant and longing look.

He wouldn't fail. In a few hours, she would be obliviously asleep, and he would have everything prepared. With a hand in his pocket, fingers curled around the key card, he shoved out the door. The cold air sliced through him and sharpened the edges of his resolve.

✧ ✧ ✧

Three hours later…

SOMETHING HEAVY PRESSED down on Joni's chest, nudging her from sleep. She dragged her eyes open.

Hazy layers of darkness smudged the outline of a man, the silhouette of his face inches from hers. No, that couldn't be right. How the hell had he gotten past her safeguards?

The familiar woodsy musk of cologne chased away her drowsiness. She bucked beneath the immovable weight, blinking rapidly, arms and legs hemmed in by bedding and the body above her.

A scream tore through her throat and garbled against the salty, hot palm clasped over her mouth. Fingers dug into her cheek. Her lungs launched into a fit of spasms, stretching her nostrils and pumping her chest in a bid for more air.

Her eyes adjusted, taking in the strong lines that sharpened his jaw. Thick lashes edged gray eyes. She knew those eyes. They'd glinted ice blue in the low-lit ambiance of the coffee shop. She'd fallen asleep fantasizing about them.

His ragged breaths heightened her own. She arched her back, tried to knock him off. Jerked her arms. No wiggle room. His knees bracketed the outsides of hers, and the tops of his feet hooked her ankles.

"Deep breaths, Joni." A kiss of whiskey traced his whisper.

Oh God, had he gotten drunk before he decided to use the key card she'd lured him with? How had he gotten past the alarm system rigged on her door or her colleague waiting in another room in the hotel?

She glared at him and growled low in her throat, her words indiscernible against his hand. *Release me, motherfucker.*

He stuffed a towel in her mouth, drowning her roar in the scratchy material. She twisted and flailed anew, succeeding only in exhausting her tension-strained body.

Smoothing her hair from her face, he spoke in a

rumbling tone. "I can see the questions wheeling in your eyes." His soft timbre contrasted with the rigid tension in his body. Uncertainty clouded the depths of his eyes, and his limbs vibrated with some kind of internal battle. He blinked, clearing it, and held up a pair of felt-lined cuffs. "I'm going to restrain—"

She shook her head, hard and fast, her tongue pushing uselessly at the terrycloth.

"Stop, Joni, and listen." The steel of his eyes sliced through her, stilling her. "I am going to restrain you; then you are going to hear my proposition."

The beat of her blood thundered in her ears. Proposition? One that she could accept or decline? Doubt shuddered through her, and she tried to engage her logic with a deep inhale. This was the guy she'd so badly wanted to go home with, and she would have under different circumstances. But he didn't know who she was or the true intentions of her interview.

The impulse to scream weakened under the gravity of how this would play out. She had liked him, *really* liked him, but he'd taken the bait and stolen her key. His job was as good as finished. If he took this much further, unemployment would be the least of his worries. She needed to talk him out of whatever he had planned. She pleaded with her eyes, tried to turn her muffles into words. *Remove the gag.*

His attention sharpened on the vicinity of her arm concealed by the bedding, and he wrestled it free. She fought, but it was an unmatched struggle. He was twice her size, quicker, and trained to subdue with a skill honed in the police academy. Within a few minutes, her arms and legs were shackled and tied to the bed frame. Restraints he'd apparently set up while she slept.

He flicked on the lamp, and light drenched the room. She lay stretched in an X on her back, chest heaving, her voice strangled by the towel. The sheets were somewhere on the floor, lost in the scuffle.

He stood at the foot of the bed, hands in his jeans pockets, buttoned shirt untucked and loose at the collar. "You always sleep in a sports bra and shorts?"

Shit, shit, shit. She'd been assigned a local operative to back her up, and damn it, she'd spoken to him before she'd fallen asleep. Everything had been in place. The alarm should've sounded in both of their rooms. Where the fuck was Agent Garcia?

Dev reached in his back pocket and held up a pocketknife. The room shrank, constricting all the oxygen, accelerating the pump of her lungs. He knelt between her spread thighs and trailed the dull edge of the blade from her navel to her sports bra.

She shuddered, her fear of the weapon warring with her anticipation of what he planned to do with it. Maybe she was thick in the head, but she believed, to the hammering depths of her heart, that he wouldn't hurt her.

He slid the steel point beneath her sports bra and cut. Sweat trickled down the back of her neck, and her body froze. What if he slipped?

The angles of his masculine jaw locked with tension, his whiskered cheeks flexing with the grind of his teeth. "Relax. I won't cut you." He sliced through both straps and removed the material.

Heat liquefied her body, from the adrenaline surging through her blood, from the way he was staring at her bared breasts. He shifted downward, cut off her shorts, and returned the knife to his back pocket.

She released a breath, her thighs flexing, stretched open and held down.

His gaze stroked every inch of her nudity and came to a stop on her pussy. "Jesus," he rasped. "You're fucking gorgeous."

The man knew how to send a thrilling shiver through her, whether she wanted it or not. He could do it just by flashing those intense blue eyes. His blond hair, long on top, shaved on the sides, formed a messy spike of bangs and framed the hard lines of his striking features. He was insanely attractive. And dangerous. She bit down on the towel.

"I'm not going to rape you, Joni." The iron resolve in his voice sank her into the mattress, overpowering her like the ropes on her arms and legs. "Nod if you understand."

In her five-year stint in Internal Affairs, she'd never miscalculated in an investigation. After her assessment of him in the coffee shop, she'd concluded he walked a precarious line of the law. She trusted his intentions not to rape her, but her instincts rioted against the chance he might lose control and force her.

She nodded but gave one of her restrained arms a pointed glare.

"You're restrained because it excites me." He fisted his hands on the mattress between her feet, his upper body braced on his arms, his eyes piercing places inside her he shouldn't be able to reach. "And because it excites you too."

The bed warmed beneath her, wrapping tendrils of heat around her, cinching her body in a fevered embrace. She'd wanted him when he'd kissed her in the shop, but her investigation and her ambivalence prohibited it. Bound and gagged, it was terrifying how much she still desired him.

"I don't want you to be afraid. That's not my thing. I want you aroused."

Her inner muscles clenched. If he fucked her without the appearance of consent, she wouldn't lose her job, wouldn't break a professional code of conduct. She tugged on the rope. Her choices had been taken from her, hadn't they? Maybe she was deluded by shock and arousal, but there was a startling amount of freedom in her restraints.

"I will not put my cock in you until you beg for it." He prowled around the bed and sat on the edge beside her hip. "I'm breaking some laws tonight, but rape isn't one of them. I've never…" He smiled crookedly and rubbed the back of his blond head. "I've never done this before."

She melted into the bed, lightened by that confirmation.

He leaned in, imprisoning her in the bluest reaches of his eyes. "If you aren't begging for it by morning, I'm yours to punch, kick, haul off to jail, and utterly destroy."

His expression was neither regretful nor cruel. Dark eyebrows made his hard eyes even more determined. A shiver ran down her spine.

"If I succeed…" He bent his head and skimmed his lips over her jaw, his sultry exhale rousing goose bumps down her neck. "If you beg me to fuck you…" His tongue swiped over her earlobe. He leaned back, snagged her eyes. "Then I will fuck you."

The crudeness in his language should've renewed her struggle against the cuffs. Instead, it sent a wave of pulsations through her clit. What if she didn't have the willpower to fight his seduction? Suddenly, the gag was a comforting restraint, a barrier to prevent her from begging.

He stood and unbuttoned his shirt, his watchful eyes holding hers hostage. Each button exposed an inch of tight skin, another crest of muscle. When the shirt dropped to the floor, he freed the button on his jeans and slid down the zipper.

The throb between her legs beat to the pound of her heart. She could ignore it. Yep, ignoring it. Ignore. Ignore. Ignore.

He shoved his pants and underwear to his feet, and

his cock jutted up, hard, thick and glistening at the tip. Good God, she couldn't look away. A blaze of desire heated her sex, lubricating her for penetration. Fucking hell, he could slide right in.

He circled the base of his girth with a finger and thumb, palm out, and stroked the length slowly. Another stroke. He regarded her, the seam of his mouth separating, his shoulders rolling forward. "Do you want this?"

She glared at him, her pussy convulsing.

A grin spread over his face, illuminating his eyes. Kneeling between her legs, he leaned in on his elbows, his knuckles just a nudge away from grazing her slit. Her hips rolled, and fuck him, he chuckled.

His head dipped, his eyes searing her needy flesh. Could he see the contractions in her inner muscles? Was her clitoris swollen and flushed? She panted around the towel.

"You have a tiny little clit, and your cunt is sopping." He drew in a long, deep breath, and his eyes shuttered, opened. "Fuck, you smell like sex and sugar."

It was too much. He was too close. She jerked against the shackles and gnawed on the gag.

He climbed up her body, still not touching her, and pinched the towel in her mouth. "You are not going to scream, because you don't want to. Trust me, Joni."

She trusted his intentions, not his control.

He yanked the gag free. She widened her jaw, wiggled it side to side. "Are you drunk?"

The silken caress of his chuckle enveloped her. "Had a couple shots of fortitude."

Drinking and driving, breaking and entering, holding her hostage…he was so fucking screwed. "You could have any woman. A *willing* woman." With his looks alone, he could walk into a bar and snap his fingers. "Why are you doing this?"

His mouth hovered a kiss away, their breaths swirling. "To seduce someone so unlawfully she pleads despite herself, to win her so thoroughly she won't turn me in"—he closed his eyes, inhaled—"is the essence of my fantasies." His eyes opened, hard and unrelenting. "I want you to share it with me, and whatever the outcome, you are worth the punishment."

The sincerity in his words, as fucked up as they were, scrambled her convictions. She wanted to scream *no*. She wanted to beg *yes*. She didn't know what to do.

He studied her, his eyes roaming her mouth, hair, throat, returning to her lips. His hands were planted on either side of her head, trembles skittering down his arms, and the hard tip of his cock tapped against her thigh.

The way he looked at her, the vehemence of his desire was an effective tactic. His mouth parted, and his slack bottom lip begged to be suckled. She lifted her head, her limbs shaking to close the distance. Captured in the dominating trap of his eyes, she felt altogether owned. It both scared and titillated her.

"Few things are more arousing"—he brushed his lips

over hers—"than breaking the rules and smudging the lines while smiling into the narrowed stare of the law."

She startled. Did he know who she was? She bit her lip. No, her investigation was confidential. The uncertainty dimmed, but it left a lingering fear. What would he do if he found out?

He shifted to kneel between her legs, his muscular thighs sliding beneath her spread ones. The side of his mouth kicked up as he gripped his cock and began to stroke. With his eyes on hers, the speed of his stroking accelerated.

Her skin quivered, yearning to be beneath the hard, desperate rub of that hand, at the center of his attention. The more he stroked, the shorter and tighter the movement became. His gaze flitted between her face and the apex of her thighs, lingering longer and longer on the latter. She absorbed the heat in his expression. She wanted him to fall over her, sink between her folds, and thrust his length to the root. Her pussy squeezed, her hips shifting up.

They stared at one another, panting. The desire in his eyes swept a trail of fire to her womb, electrifying every nerve ending in its path. "I get off on you watching me, Joni." Ragged breaths tumbled from his lips. "Do you like what you see?"

"You're an exhibitionist." And damn it, her breathy response gave him his answer.

"Just horny, Joni." His abs contracted as his hips thrust against his hand. The corner of his mouth pulled up. "You and your labels."

Gorgeous. Seductive. Unlawful. He vibrated with labels. The twisting and compressing of his fist and the beauty and raw power of his strong body nearing climax propelled her pelvis into a rocking motion.

All that toned flesh slick with sweat, his chest and abs flexing and straining for release built an explosive pressure in her core. She wanted him, but if she begged him, what part would she be playing in his twisted game? What would she write in her report? He broke into her room, tied her up, and she begged him to fuck her? She would lose her job.

His mouth hung open, gasping. He jerked his fist up and down along his cock and caught his forward lean with a hand beside her hip. Groaning, he gave himself the relief he so desperately needed. She moaned with him as he pumped stream after stream of warm come on her belly.

She squeezed her eyes shut, her body humming for her own release.

"Hey, man." At the sound of his voice, her eyes flew open. Phone to his ear, he shoved the towel back in her mouth.

What the hell? Her shocked glare was a wasted effort as he paced toward the door, muscles flexing in his tight ass. "We're ready." He disconnected and tossed the phone on a nearby table.

Ice shot through her veins. Was someone coming to the room? She twisted and writhed as the bastard kept his back to her.

A few minutes later, he opened the door. A handsome Hispanic man strode through, brown eyes as bright as his smile. Dev shook his hand and led him into the room.

A drug dealer? Male prostitute? Hired hit man? A tumult of nerves stiffened the hairs on her arms.

The man stripped his clothes on the way to the bed. Waxed, oiled, and toned, his dark skin glistened in the lamplight. A male prostitute.

She tried to close her legs. Of course, she fucking couldn't. She should've screamed when she had the chance. Her heart rate doubled, and her breaths rushed loud and wet through her nose.

"Do you know who this is, Joni?" Dev strode past him, unabashed in his nudity, his cock hardening again.

She shook her head, pretending that her gaping, soaked pussy wasn't broadcasting *fuck me* to the too-crowded room of naked men.

The stranger dropped to his knees beside the bed and smirked. "I'm Agent Manuel Garcia. Sorry I'm late."

She stopped breathing, her head spinning with objections. No no no. He was lying.

Dev ran a finger over the arch of her foot, drawing her attention. "Manuel's an old friend of mine. He tipped me off a couple hours ago, got me past the alarm system." He tsked. "Setting me up, Joni?"

Her stomach dropped. Manuel was supposed to

protect her, not betray her to Dev.

Dev's hand slid up her leg, leaving a shiver of goose bumps. "So my exhibitionism in New Orleans aroused Internal Affairs' suspicion about my extracurricular activities, yeah?"

Yeah. The guy he'd fucked in a crowded club had learned who he was and reported him. It had been consensual, albeit messy for someone in Dev's profession, which was why the bureau had sent her.

"Good thing Manuel owes me a favor." His velvet laugh made her blood boil and nipples tighten. "I would've fallen right into your trap."

Instead, she'd fallen into his. Her back arched, and she moaned against the towel.

As if their movements had been choreographed, Manuel rolled a condom over Dev's length without uttering a word. When the man proceeded to deep throat him, everything in her went completely still.

Dev palmed the back of Manuel's head and guided the speed of the sucking. His heavy-lidded eyes, the slack of his jaw, and the grind of his hips communicated unbridled lust. The way they moved together reeked of sexual familiarity. Was he gay? Was he using her only as a voyeur to satisfy his kink to be watched?

Frustration coiled between her legs, and a quivering exhale escaped her tight throat.

Dev looked up, and his smoldering expression made her thighs tremble, sweeping a tingle to her toes. He dragged his gaze to her cunt, to the damp heat that promised a smooth and pleasurable glide of his girth.

"Stand up and turn around." Dev tapped Manuel's jaw and held her eyes. "Do you want my cock?"

She was certain he was addressing her, but Manuel answered as he stood and turned, "Fuck, yes."

Dev applied the lube he'd retrieved from his bag and gripped the other man's hips. With a few prods of his cock, Dev seated himself to the root. They shuddered in unison.

Their position, she realized, was for her vantage. The profiles and curvature of their muscular bodies rolling as one set off an explosion of sensations through her body. The pounding beat of desire concentrated between her legs and spread outward, shivering over her belly and tightening her nipples. Her breasts felt heavy and full, jogging with the heave of her chest.

Manuel pulled on his dick in desperate jerks, and Dev controlled the pace of their rocking, lips tracing the rigid lines of Manuel's shoulder. It was beautiful and erotic, and her body responded as if she were there between them, bowing and trembling and glistening with sweat. Her lungs labored to keep up.

Two pairs of eyes roamed her face, then narrowed on the spasmodic flex of her cunt. She yanked at the tethers, needed her hands to assuage the chaos of pulsations assaulting her pussy. She ground her ass against the bed, sliding in the wet spot.

"She wants us to fuck her." Manuel accelerated the slapping motion of his fist, his head turning to capture

Dev's mouth. They licked aggressively, lips spread wide, tongues warring and flicking.

Dev broke the kiss, met her eyes. "Do you want Manuel to fuck you?"

Sweat dampened her lip and forehead. Her pulse roared in her ears. Fuck, she was burning with the need for Dev to touch her, to pump his fingers in and out and massage that place that would release her from this urgency.

"Remove her gag." Dev slid a hand over her thigh, and the heat from his skin licked a fiery path along her slit. She clung to the lust in his eyes and the noisy gasps stumbling from his lips.

When Manuel pulled the towel from her mouth, she was mindless, hips circling in the air, empty, so fucking empty. "Please tell me you're not gay."

A sensual smile tipped the corners of his mouth, and he thrust his hips, curling his fingers inside her. "Horny, Joni."

Arrgh. She needed to reestablish the lines, remind him she was Internal Affairs and they would both be arrested, but that wasn't what came out. "Fuck me. Please, I want you to fuck me."

"Me or him?" Dev rotated his pelvis against the arch of Manuel's ass and traced two fingers around the opening of her pussy.

Every minute movement was a jolt of electricity. "You. I want you. Deeper." She lifted her ass, tried to grind her folds against his touch. "Please, Dev."

His fingers tunneled in, slipping to the knuckles,

launching her higher, higher, toward the precipice. Waves of pleasure built, strengthening with each stroke along her inner muscles. The tang of her arousal chased her inhales. Moisture seeped around his hand and leaked down the crack of her ass. Just a few more thrusts—

The fingers vanished, returning to Manuel's hip.

"No, please." Beyond the edges of her desperation whispered a scolding voice, *Stop begging.* She didn't care. She didn't want him to reach his crest with that man. She balled her hands and lowered her chin and her voice. "Fuck me, Dev."

He pressed his lips against Manuel's nape, and for an ice-cold second, she thought he'd rejected her. He raised his hand and smacked the man's ass. "Consider your debt paid." He pulled out and discarded the condom.

The pressure swelling her sex and the rope holding her down were a combined hell. As Manuel dressed, she jerked and pulled on the restraints until Dev crawled between her legs, his shoulders pressed against her thighs. She tumbled into the steel cage of his eyes, and his grip on her waist told her he was teetering on an equally tortured edge.

He lowered his head and circled his tongue around her clit. Silk and heat. Wet and desire. She devoured that first touch of his mouth on her sensitive flesh. The movements were slow, controlled, propelling her to the top of the tide where her release gathered, waiting for a spectacular crash.

The door slammed shut, and Dev sat on his heels,

leaving a chill in the absence of his mouth. "I need to wash up. Be right back."

"No, wait." She didn't want to be alone with her thoughts. Didn't want a single second to doubt.

He disappeared behind the bathroom door, the fucking sadist. The *whoosh* of the faucet filtered through the room. Was he purposefully giving her time to cool down?

She closed her eyes, her body thrumming for relief. If his aim was to show her the thin and perilous line between seduction and coercion, he'd succeeded. He'd violated a number of laws to seduce her, and his approach could very well be considered coercion through compulsion and duress.

When she opened her eyes, he was standing at the foot of the bed, jaw loose, abs contracting, his cock long and hard in his hand. Her pulse raced.

In the next heartbeat, he was on her, straddling her waist, eating at her mouth. His whiskers scratched her chin as he dragged his lips over hers. The steel bar of his erection slid a trail of fire along her belly.

His hands framed her face, and he kissed with such ardor, the whip of his tongue so relentless and consuming she felt it in every fiber of her body. Her blood heated, grateful and greedy, as she tried to match his pace. He reached for the cuffs on her wrists, her arms pulled free, the intensity of his kisses unyielding.

Then he raised his head, mouth puffy and wet worry lines creasing the corners of his eyes. He slid backward and flicked the quick release on each of her ankles.

She lifted her hands, pulled her legs together, the pang of reality slamming into her chest. She was free. Was that it? He was done with her?

He knelt on the edge of the bed, an unreadable expression softening his prominent jaw. "Whatever you decide to do, I have no regrets. Watching you soar to such a glorious high was worth the consequence."

Whatever she decided to do? Her swollen lips tickled at the edges, and she leaped on him, squeezing her thighs around his hips. He landed on his back, his hands skidding over her breasts, their mouths locked in desperation. His urgency burned hers to an unbearable fever.

She curled her fingers around his steel length and rasped, "Condom."

He pointed at his duffel bag even as his cock prodded her opening.

Fuck. The separation from his body heat was torture, but she returned swiftly, unrolling the latex with trembling hands. By the time she climbed atop him, he was flexing his ass and fucking the air between them.

Hovering above him, her smile caught in the bite of her teeth, she lined up her body and slid down his length. The exquisite stretch of his girth bowed her back and swallowed her thoughts, her oxygen, her entire world.

He let out a groan. "Fuuuuck, Joni." The hot grip of his hands covered her ass, controlling the movement of her hips as he rocked himself inside of her.

The powerful strokes of his cock spiraled a frenzy of

sensations through her. She leaned forward and curled her tongue into his mouth, reaching deep, trying to consume him, to own him, but he took over.

He was ravenous, working his tongue against hers, furiously licking, sucking, devouring her lips. He kneaded her breasts, his balls slapping against her ass with each ruthless thrust. Her head swam in mindless pleasure. They were passion and fire, wanton and reckless. She was undone.

The coil of tension in her pussy unraveled, firing sparks through her body and flexing her toes. She threw her head back and let it go. "Ahhhh, Dev. I'm coming. Oh God. Fuck, fuck, fuck…"

As her shoulders continued to hitch and shudder, he flipped her to her back and fucked her hard and fast. A moment later, he shouted through his climax.

They collapsed on their sides, face-to-face, breathing noisily, sharing sated smiles. He drew her to his chest, and within a few minutes, his eyes drifted closed and his breathing deepened.

She stretched to the side of the bed that met the wall and retrieved her handcuffs from beneath the mattress.

Eyes closed, he murmured, "You're unlawful in bed, Joni."

She looked at the cuffs in her hand, looked at his confident, sleepy face, and grinned.

Want more from Pam Godwin? You can read DIRTY TIES, a standalone romantic suspense.

Captivated

Cynthia Rayne

"YOU NEVER TOLD me your name."

I glanced in the rearview mirror to see my prisoner, Jonathan Royal, studying my reflection from behind the metal bars that separated us. Despite the orange jumpsuit, he was a looker. Thick black hair, soulful brown eyes, a full sensual mouth, and a squared jaw. Born and raised in Alabama, he had impeccable manners and exuded charm by the bucket load.

Well, as much a killer could.

I focused on the road once more. It was truly a bone-chilling January night and I had to watch for patches of slick black ice on the overpasses. "As far as you're concerned, my name is Deputy Marshal or ma'am. Take your pick."

"Just figured we could get more familiar since we are on a road trip and all, *ma'am*."

"We aren't going on a ski trip, Royal. This is a prison transport." Prisoners always underestimated me, particularly men. I could see why. At five-two with a curvy build, long red hair and wide blue eyes, I looked more like a Sunday school teacher than a threat. But he should know appearances could be deceiving. I'd taken on guys nearly twice my size and won.

"All I want to know is your name. That's all. Hardly seems fair, since you know everything about me from my jacket. Why," he drawled, "I bet you know my height, weight, birthday, and exact locations and detailed descriptions of each and every single one of my tattoos." He whispered that last part, a husky little vocal caress that felt like it had been purred into my ear.

I shivered, and not from the cold seeping in my windowpane either.

Damn it. Why couldn't he be some ugly old guy? I shouldn't even be alone with him. Since the recession the marshal service had gone through a series of debilitating cutbacks. Normally two marshals would be transporting someone as dangerous as Royal and he'd be stuffed and cuffed in the back of a gas-guzzling van, so I'd only have to see him at the beginning and end of the trip. Now only a few thin bars separated us, and I didn't have a partner with me. Someone else I could talk to. So much easier to pretend the prisoner didn't exist when I could bullshit about weather and bad coffee on the road with a fellow officer.

"If I were you? I would keep my mouth closed and quit while I was ahead. Looks to me like you got a pretty sweet deal, transferring from a maximum security prison to minimum for being such a good boy. Going to be like Club Fed for you. I hear at McCreary they have a prisoner-run garden and even a recue dog program. It's going to be like going to college. Why do you want to risk your oh so *exemplary* record by harassing me?"

"Now that is a conundrum worth pondering. Perhaps you make me lose control, Ms. Marshal."

I scowled at him in the mirror.

Royal cocked a brow at me. "Have to admit, I wouldn't mind your hands on me once more. I've been in prison ten long and lonely years. No conjugal visits. No female visitors that weren't related to me. Been a long time since I've even been in the same room with a woman. And here we are, just the two of us. Intimate quarters." He strained in his steel bonds, getting closer to me, closing his eyes as he breathed me in. "Even the smell of your perfume tempts me."

Jesus. He did have a way with words. Evidently my body had just taken a vacation from sanity, because I began to respond to his sweet talk, a treacherous warmth spreading through me. I bit down on my lower lip viciously, trying to drag my thoughts in another direction. I needed to get it together, pronto.

This whole evening was a bit of a shit show. I'd been out on a date with Tim, a high school math teacher I couldn't quite decide if I liked or not, when I'd been called in. The marshal who had been scheduled to take Royal had come down with the flu, and I had the misfortune to answer my cell. I'd made my excuses, changed out my low-cut red sweater and tight jeans for a respectable pair of khakis and a white button-down, though I still wore makeup and perfume. On the job I made an effort to appear androgynous so I didn't attract any more attention than I already did.

Time to put this guy in his place.

"If you don't shut the fuck up, Royal, I'm going to gag you. Or throw your sorry ass in the trunk," I threatened. That would so be worth having a letter in my file over.

Due to being pissed off, I turned a curve a little too fast, and the car swerved. Goddamn black ice. I immediately stepped off the gas and turned into the skid, the quickest way to regain control.

But it didn't work.

The car began to spin, doing a slow one eighty, circling round and round until we rammed headfirst into the concrete wall in the median.

I was lucky enough to be thrown into the airbag, but Royal's head banged into the steel bars. Thankfully we weren't going very fast because I'd stepped off the gas.

"You okay?" I asked Royal, glancing in the rearview.

He blinked a few times and shook his head. "Rung my bell pretty good, but I'm fine. Though I'm gonna have a pounding headache tomorrow." Didn't have a mark on him. Good. We were both okay, but the car had been crunched up by the concrete pretty good. We weren't going anywhere anytime soon.

I picked up my cell and dialed the boss. "Sir? It's Blake. Got into an accident on the highway."

"Shit. You okay?" I liked my boss, Harry Walters.

Efficient, loved the job, and no nonsense.

"Yes. Prisoner and I are just fine. Going to call the highway patrol and report the accident, then haul his ass to the county jail for the night. Maybe we could requisition a car from the troopers so I can finish the job?"

"I'll cut through the red tape and give you a call in about thirty. Keep me updated." He paused. "Blake, if he tries anything, you put him down and you put him down hard. Don't trust him for a second."

"Got it, sir. I'll keep you updated." I hung up and dialed the staties. Told them what mile marker we were located at.

Then I turned to actually face Royal. It was unnerving. Even after the accident, he didn't seem flustered. Just calm. Those dark eyes of his drank me in. Missed nothing.

"Hold tight. They will be here in a few to get us. We got top priority."

"Tell me, Ms. Blake—"

"Eavesdropping, were we?"

"Can I help it if your supervisor has a voice that carries? Tell me, are you a Ms. or Mrs. Blake? I would hate to think I had a rival for your affections."

I rolled my eyes. "Enough already. I'm having the night from hell, and your incessant need to talk isn't making it better. So I'm going to tell you and then you are going to shut up about it, okay?" He nodded, but I doubt he intended to keep his promise. "My name is Ivy

Blake. And I'm not a Mrs."

"And do you have a boyfriend?"

"No, I have a girlfriend," I lied. Let him chew on that one for a bit.

He threw back his head and laughed. "I don't think you are telling me the truth, but we have another problem. Upon closer examination, it appears a bruise is forming on my temple." He bobbed his head to the mirror.

I could see a small dark red circle above his left eyebrow. I thought it was just a scratch, but I didn't think blowing off a prisoner's potential head injury would be great for my career.

"Perhaps you could check my forehead? Make sure I am not more seriously injured?" he suggested.

I froze. No way was I going to open the cage and check his face out myself. That sounded like a one-way ticket to being shot in the gut and left in a ditch. Truthfully, I wanted to dump his ass on the front lawn of McCreary and get the hell back home. Not an option though. "Yeah, I only have basic first-aid training, but I will get a professional to clear you." I called the state patrol once more and told them to send an ambulance as well.

And then I saw the headlights of an oncoming vehicle.

Moving fast, headed straight for us. No time to get away. A van slammed into the passenger side, throwing Royal and I into the windows and steamrolling the car fifty yards down the road in a shower of sparks and burned rubber. Two men dressed all in black with ski masks over their faces sprang from the van, moving toward the car with purpose.

"Oh shit!" Not. An. Accident.

I grabbed for my Glock and rolled my window down so they could hear me. "I am a United States deputy marshal. Keep your distance from the vehicle and put your weapons down!" I shouted. They both brandished sawed-off shotguns. Not a fair fight.

"They are here for you, aren't they?" I never took my eyes off the men.

I could almost hear his smile. "Why, yes, they are."

Thought as much. "Tell me, is this the execution squad or the welcome wagon?"

"I believe these gentlemen are friends of mine from the days prior to my unfortunate incarceration."

The men kept approaching, and they aimed at me. "That thing might as well be a peashooter," the tallest said. "We could blow a hole in you from here."

He was right. They would open fire, and I would just be a red mess in the front seat. "Yeah, but then you might hit your friend here. We'd both be decorating the seats."

"Enough," Royal said, exasperated. "No one is getting shot. Ms. Blake here has no doubt determined that putting up a fight would lead to her demise. Since she is a smart woman, she is going to throw down her weapon." I stared at him, and I could swear I saw a pleading look in his eyes. "Why don't you toss your weapon out the window, and these good gentlemen will collect it for you. That way everyone gets to live."

"Everyone?" I hesitated.

"I swear to you. Everyone is going to survive this."

I gritted my teeth, tried my best to hide the fear clawing at my insides. I must be crazy, because I believed him. The gun felt good in my hands, like a steel safety blanket. But I was smart enough to know when to part with it. With a curse I chucked it out onto the pavement. "You are taking me hostage instead of killing me. Smart."

Royal had been selling guns and running drugs for nearly five years when he'd gotten picked up in a RICO investigation. He'd been the president of Kentucky's Four Horsemen chapter, part of a national outlaw biker gang. Someone with that kind of power and influence had a good head on his shoulders. Killing a federal agent would bring a lot of unwanted heat. Using me as a bargaining tool would give him a lot of options.

"Don't be so negative, Ms. Blake. Hostage is such an ugly word. You will be my guest."

"Look, you can call me a guest or, hell, your date if you want to, but keep in mind that kidnapping is still a felony and you've already racked up quite a few of those. Extortion. Illegal arms sales. Murder. Assault. Racketeering."

The van drivers yanked open my car door and dragged me out of the vehicle, dumping me on the chilly blacktop. I let my body go limp, not impeding their progress but not helping either. I didn't fight or give them a reason to rough me up.

Be cool. Calm. I took long, deep breaths.

They reached for my belt and removed the keys hooked to it. The short one fastened my own handcuffs around my wrists. The tall one went to the sedan, unlocked the rear door, then released Royal from his restraints. They hauled me to my feet and escorted both of us to the vehicle.

Royal reached across the backseat and laid a hand on my cheek, smoothing it. "Are you okay, Ivy?"

"Just ducky." I notched my chin higher, a little bit of a *fuck you* in my demeanor. Truthfully? I was scared spitless, but I'd be damned if I'd admit to it.

He laughed. "I admire your fortitude. You are a very brave woman, but then you would have to be to pursue this line of work."

"Yeah, right about now I'm wishing I would have followed my mom's footsteps instead of my father's and become a preschool teacher."

Royal's goons put the pedal to the metal, and we screeched away from the crash scene. My mind raced, but eventually my training kicked in. I noted our direction and the passing mile markers. And anything else that might be helpful to investigators.

Royal withdrew a leather pouch from a compartment in the car and removed a vial and needle from it. I inched closer to my window, but there was nowhere to go in the confined space. He patiently loaded the needle, then flicked it with his thumb to remove any air bubbles.

It never occurred to me that the assholes would shoot me full of drugs. Blow to the head? Maybe.

He reached for my arm, and I jerked away. *Oh Christ.* "What the hell is that?"

His voice was slow and soothing. "Just a little sedative. I asked the boys to bring it with them. Much more efficient way of knocking you unconscious. Never know when it might come in handy."

"You can blindfold me or, um—"

"There is no telling what you might pick up, just from listening. I'm truly sorry to have to drug you, but I can't have you remembering the exact location of my hideout, can I?"

"I—"

He reached for my arm again, and I didn't struggle this time. The fight would come later. "Don't open your mouth and lie to me. There won't be any lies between us, Ivy. Not ever," he warned as he shoved the needle in.

I didn't like the way he kept using my name or how intently he watched me.

And with that last thought, I tumbled into blackness.

✧ ✧ ✧

WHAT THE HELL?

I had cotton mouth, and my head pounded like a

stampede of horses had just clomped over it. Not ponies either; big fucking Clydesdales. Hadn't felt this bad since the morning after my twenty-first birthday. I forced my eyes open, but I felt dizzy. Room spun around me, and my surroundings weren't familiar. Scratchy blanket beneath my cheek and I slept on a bed with a quilt. Space heater beside the bed. I didn't own one.

Then it hit me.

I shot up. That's right. I was being held captive by Royal and two of his MC brothers, who would remain anonymous until I personally yanked their ski masks off and hauled their sorry asses to jail. I glanced down. Thankfully I was still fully clothed; no one had gotten molesty on me while I visited dreamland.

"Good morning, sunshine."

I startled, turning around to see Royal in a small kitchen a few feet from me. He had changed out of his prison jumpsuit in favor of a pair of blue jeans and a black cable-knit sweater. He looked more like a model than a criminal in his street clothes.

I started piecing together our new location. Wooden doors, wooden floors, wooden walls, and even the ceiling. We were in a cabin, not a hotel room. Definitely close quarters. One queen-size bed, a fireplace, a couch, and a tiny kitchen. There was another door that I assumed led to a bathroom.

"You slept nearly twenty-four hours. Would you like some coffee? I just made some. I'd offer you food, but my companions thought provisions meant bags of Cheetos and Spam." He sighed. "I never thought I'd long for prison food again."

"I'll pass on the Cheetos, but I'll take coffee with cream and sugar." God, I needed coffee. Hopefully that would help me out of my stupor. I watched him prepare it, lest he shake in any "special" ingredients that would put me to sleep again, then made my way to the couch.

I sat, pressing a hand to my forehead as though I could keep it from pounding. "So does this cabin belong to you? Maybe you hunted in northern Kentucky during the fall?" I peered out the window and saw only woods around us and snow, which fell at a good clip. At this rate we would be getting a couple of inches an hour. Bet the weather hindered the manhunt too. Slowing down the vehicles, covering any tracks.

Had to hand it to Royal. Laying low in a place that wouldn't be investigated was a damn good plan. A hunting cabin in an isolated forest fit the bill. Standard procedure was to patrol highways, airports, and other modes of transportation to chase down a fugitive. They wouldn't be tromping through the woods without good reason.

He laughed as he handed me the coffee, then sat on the sofa beside me. "Yes, this is a cabin. No, it is not mine."

I thought for just a moment about throwing the hot liquid at him, making a run for it, but I needed more information. Where were his cronies? Did he have a vehicle I could swipe? Or did he dump the van and hoof it here? He also handed me a bottle of aspirin, and I gulped down two of them.

He set his cup down on the table in front of us. "Decided against scalding me, huh?"

Evidently I shouldn't be a poker player. I smiled, showing a row of sharp and shiny teeth. "For now."

"That brings us to our current predicament. I can't have you trying to incapacitate me and making a run for it. We have several options to solve that particular problem."

I nearly choked as I imagined the worst way to solve it.

He grinned. "Ivy, if I wanted to harm you, I would have done so after I got free. I meant what I said. I'm not going to kill you."

I was probably going to kick myself for asking this question. "Why didn't you?"

He looked offended. "I don't harm innocent people. I know what you must think of me, but I'm not a monster. I have killed men, yes, but only in the due course of my business. All of these men lived in my world and knew its rules. While it may appear lawless to outsiders, there are many guidelines you never break. Killing without provocation and harming women and children are unacceptable."

Oh, lucky me, I got taken hostage by the sensitive psychopath.

Sounded like a lot of bullshit justification to me, but

he seemed sincere about his twisted moral code of sorts. I guessed for now I'd just be grateful I hadn't landed on his shit list. "How do you propose to solve this problem?"

"I could keep you tied up, but that is inconvenient. I don't think it's the right tone for our relationship."

Color me confused. "Um, Royal, we don't have a relationship. Unless you mean the hostage/kidnapper kind of bond."

"Ah, that's where you are wrong. It's just brand-new and needs to be nurtured, so I don't want to break the trust by manhandling you."

He laid his arm across the back of the couch, directly behind my head, and I shifted, moving closer to the edge of my seat. "I think the trust is already broken by the kidnapping."

He smiled. "I told you, you are my guest. Not a hostage."

"You say tomato; I say hostage." I shrugged. "So what is your solution?"

"Well, I don't want to drug you either. It really isn't good to have that many sedatives coursing through that delicious body of yours at one time."

I let the delicious comment slide. "And? Spill it. I'm getting older here." He seemed to be dragging his metaphorical feet on this one.

"The only option I see is stripping you down until you're bare," he said, his voice slipping to a darker register. "That way you won't be tempted to make a run for it."

I could feel the sexual tension curl between us once more, and I tried like hell to tamp it down. Ignore it. "Come again?" He'd clearly lost his mind.

"It is the best solution. It won't harm you. The weather will be your jailor, not me. You wouldn't make it more than a few minutes without frostbite. So, if you don't mind," he said, gesturing to my clothing.

"Hmm. Funnily enough? I *do* mind stripping off my clothing in front of a strange man. I'm not taking my clothes off." I wrapped my arms around my chest and glowered at him.

His face went frighteningly calm. Like it had been when he'd shot me up with a sedative. This was going to happen whether I wanted it to or not. "Yes, Ivy. You are."

"Said the date rapist," I rejoined.

He sighed. "You saw my file. I have not stooped to raping a woman, and I never will. However, I will drug you again, and that will be that, if you so choose."

I didn't let it go or back down. "Didn't you make the creepy comment about wanting my hands on you while we were driving?"

"That comment wasn't creepy. It was flirtatious," he countered. "And what's more? You thought so too. I saw the blush on your cheeks. Besides, I said I wanted *your* hands on me. I didn't threaten to put *my* hands on you."

He had an answer for everything.

He sighed. "I had hoped you would choose the most rational option. You would rather the drugs again?"

"No!" I could see there was no way out of this. I had less of a chance of escaping if I was knocked unconscious. "Where are your two goons?"

He chuckled. "My *associates* have gone elsewhere to disappear for a while. It is just the two of us, Ivy. I promise."

That was somewhat better. "Let's say, for a moment, that I do take off my clothes. You understand that is not some sort of invitation, right?" I slapped my coffee cup on the table and stood, staring down at him with what I hoped was an intimidating expression. "You come near me, and I am going to go Thunderdome on your ass. One of us won't survive, and my money is on you. Got it?" I snapped.

My threat seemed to amuse him. "I understand. Of course, that is predicated on you not wanting my attentions, but I promise to not come near until you ask me to."

"Yeah, well, don't count on it, buddy." I turned around and undid my button-down shirt. Then I unbuckled the belt on my khakis, along with the fly. With horror I realized that while I had dressed for work, I hadn't completely changed out of my date attire. I still wore a pretty pink lace bra and matching bikini panties beneath my clothes. I wasn't sure if I actually wanted to sleep with the teacher I'd gone out with, but I had given myself the option when I got dressed.

I hesitated for a moment, and then something wicked occurred to me.

He wanted me. *Really* wanted me. I could practically feel his craving. Ten years without a woman. Ten years.

He watched me undress. Missing nothing. This might be a way to escape. If I put on a little show, it would shake his control and throw him off guard. I might be able to escape then. I toed off my shoes, let my pants slide to the floor and turned to face him, crossing my arms over myself, wrapping my shirt teasingly around my body.

The distance between his legs had widened on the couch.

"You are so beautiful," he murmured, his eyes drinking me in.

I got closer, standing between his splayed thighs, and let the shirt fall open. My breasts nearly overflowed the demicup bra, and they moved in time with my breaths. I stretched behind my back, pretending to grasp the hooks and eyes, causing my breasts to jiggle a bit, and he made a strangled sound.

"I can't seem to work the clasp," I whispered and then presented him with my back. "Will you undo it?"

"Christ! You are killing me," he said through gritted teeth. "Do you know what happens to women who tease a man like that?"

I could feel a smile curling my lips. What the hell? I shouldn't be smiling. I should be terrified. I stood between a murderer's legs in little more than a few scraps of lace. But somehow I was enjoying this. Relishing teasing him, seeing the effect I had on him.

I cleared my throat, tried to keep the glee out of my voice. "I don't know about that, but I do know you promised not to touch me. Just a few minutes ago?"

"Hoisted by my own petard on this one." His hands felt big and warm on my back. He very slowly undid the two clasps that held my bra together. Then he smoothed the skin where the bra straps had bit into it. He pushed them down my arms, moving up behind me, and the garment started to pitch to the floor. I instinctively caught it, but he pried it from my fingers and let it drop. I started to wrap my arms around my breasts, but he covered them with his hands. Kneaded them, tweaking both of my nipples until they stood at attention.

Then he swept my hair to one side. I could feel his heated breath on the back of my neck. He kissed me there, just below my hairline, and I shuddered in response. How did he know I would be so sensitive there?

What was I doing? I should protest. I should demand he release me. Knee him in the balls or slap his face. Something. *Anything.* But I couldn't make myself do it. I wanted this. I don't know why, but I had been wondering how his hands would feel on me as soon as I laid eyes on him. I had to see where this led, even if the path brought me to my own ruin.

He pulled me back against him, and I could feel his

cock, pressing hard into my ass. He groaned again, a deep rumble that reverberated through my body. He undid his fly and pushed his pants down and pressed against me, closer still. His heated flesh warmed me through the thin material of my panties. He tucked his fingers in the waistband and slipped them farther down my legs and the wetness seeped from my pussy.

Royal placed his pulsing cock between my legs, abrading my wet lips. He yanked me hard against his body, arms trapping me. "Ivy, when it comes to you, I apparently can't control myself. If you don't want this, I suggest you say something now, or I won't be able to stop." He chuckled without humor. "Hell, I'm not even sure I could stop now. All I can think about is being inside you. Do you want to stop me?"

Did I? I did on some level, but I couldn't make myself speak up. The only answer I could give was rubbing against him, letting his cock slide between my slickened folds.

He howled then, bending me over a bit so he could thrust in earnest. "I. Am. Not. Going. To. Last. Long," he said, punctuating each word with a thrust that robbed me of breath. The position caused the thick head to graze my clit. I reached between my legs as he pushed into me, and played with myself as he circled my opening. With a wail, I came. As soon as I did, he slammed his cock inside me. My hands fell to the coffee table, and I gritted my teeth as he fucked me hard. With a groan he came, spilling himself inside me again and again. Filling me with his seed.

When it was over, he carried me to the bed and wrapped me in his arms. I was left staring at the ceiling, thoughts racing. I was cuddled in bed with a fugitive. A convicted felon. A murderer, for pity's sake. What had I just allowed to happen? There had been no doubt. I hadn't even pretended to not be interested. I'd wanted him. I'd tacitly agreed to it. Hell, I'd *provoked* it. But I was too good of a person to break bad at this point in my life. So what did it mean?

"You are so quiet over there," he whispered.

"Just thinking," I mumbled.

"I know." He kissed my forehead. "I can practically hear the wheels turning in that formidable brain of yours. I know any moment now the recriminations are going to come, and I can't tolerate it. I just want to lie here in the dark with you snuggled up in my arms. Hear your heartbeat next to mine, and I'm truly sorry for what I'm about to do." Once again, I felt the sharp sting of the needle.

The bastard drugged me. Again.

✧ ✧ ✧

I WOKE ONCE more to discover my hands cuffed above my head. I was lying on the queen-size bed, wearing my lacy pink panties and my white button-down shirt buttoned to my navel.

Royal must have dressed me after he'd knocked my ass out. *Speak of the evil sandman.* He cleared his throat from across the room. He was fully dressed, including a leather jacket.

"How long was I out for this time?"

"Only twelve hours. I gave you a much smaller dose."

"Aren't you a gentleman?" I narrowed my eyes. "Do that again and I won't be the only one knocked out cold."

His lips twitched. "Understood, ma'am."

I nodded to his outfit. "Going out for a stroll?"

"Police reports said they are starting to search the forest. Apparently my brothers stupidly ditched the van not too far from the woods. It's time to go." Since I was trussed half-naked to a bed, I bet he meant to go alone, without me.

"I see."

"No, I don't think you do, Ivy." Before I could blink, he was on me, hand sliding down the length of my body, neck to knees. My nipples pebbled in response, and when he rested his hand between my legs, playing with the lace, I could feel my pussy become liquid. Readying for his touch. For his inevitable invasion. "I can't take you with me now. Too much heat and you would only draw more, but I am coming back for you. I realized it when we made love. This...*obsession* I have with you isn't going anywhere. It's only going to get deeper."

I blinked. "That's crazy. We...well, I'm not sure what we did last night, but that is done and over. What

I really am is your hostage."

"What you are, Ivy, is *mine,* and don't you forget it." With that pronouncement, he plunged two fingers deep inside me. "You belong to me. We both felt that last night, and no one will keep us apart, not even the federal government." He leaned down and kissed each of my nipples in turn, punished each with a little bite. Then he claimed my mouth with his, stealing my air and causing me to undulate against his questing fingers.

He finally drew back, his breath labored. He very deliberately licked my juices from his fingertips. "I need to go before they get too close."

He buttoned my shirt, set my panties to rights, and covered my bare legs with the blankets. "I'm going to leave, Ivy, and when I'm safely away, I will leave an anonymous tip as to your whereabouts. Don't worry. You won't be here long. I would untie you, but I know you are still coming to terms with our relationship." He paused, searching my eyes. "Unless you can tell me, Ivy."

"Tell you what?" I gasped.

"That you belong to me." His dark gaze pinned me.

I opened my mouth to speak. To deny it, but somehow I couldn't say the words, nor could I say what he wanted me to. I shut my mouth, shook my head.

"That's okay. You aren't ready yet. I am a patient man, and one night in the not too distant future, you are going to wake up in my arms." He walked to the door. "See you soon, my love." And with that, he was gone.

The trouble was? I believed him. I'm just not sure whether that news filled me with dread. Or joy. Perhaps a bit of both.

SLIPKNOT

SHERI SAVILL

*L*EATHER. *SEXY AND tight. Perfect. Yep, this is the one. This is the one I'm taking.*

Mia took a deep breath and, in one smooth move, rolled and tucked the metal hanger—and the soft black leather miniskirt still clipped to it—into her black shoulder bag. Right over the open zipper and down into the gaping hole at the top of the purse, all without a hitch.

Thank God the fucking price tag didn't catch on the zipper track.

Once it was all pushed down inside the darkness of her purse, she rested the crook of her elbow over the opening again, for extra camouflage, in case prying eyes should happen to look too closely as she left the shop. Four hundreds dollars' worth? Really? The tiny skirt was easy enough to conceal. It was an obscene price for a leather mini, anyway, she rationalized. Even for a skirt as sexy and well-made as this one, that was too much money. She could smell the richness of fine leather wafting from the other skirts still on the rack in front of her as she glanced sideways again. All quiet. Not a soul in the shop but her and the guy behind the counter. And he was still gone.

God, that was really just too easy.

She felt her lips pursing together a little in spite of herself, barely suppressing her self-satisfaction. Still, no reason to be cocky. She'd planned this carefully enough in advance. Stupid thieves were always being caught because they didn't think things through, or they became too brazen, too greedy. The news was full of dumb criminal stories. She'd resolved not to be one of them.

Mia shifted her weight a little in her black heels and then took a few small steps down the aisle toward the ball gags, crops, hoods…glancing sideways again toward the cash register, now bathed in the soft greenish glow of a banker's lamp on the counter. The dimmer-than-usual lighting meant that Flesh Factory—the largest kinky sex emporium and BDSM equipment supplier in the city—was empty, about to close for the night, which was exactly what she had counted on. But even as the last customer of the day, she'd taken no chances and sent the lone employee—friendly, handsome, ever-so-helpful "Michael"—on an errand to the stockroom to check for fence-net thigh-highs she knew he wouldn't find. They didn't even carry them anymore. She knew the stripper-wear section well and pretty much owned one of everything they sold by now.

She continued to pretend to browse, exhaling another slow breath. It was exciting, breaking the law.

She'd done it. And now the leather skirt was hers. All that was left to do was make a hasty yet friendly exit shortly after Michael returned, apologetic and empty-handed, from the goose chase she'd sent him on.

The short, low-cut white dress she'd worn tonight—no bra, of course—had been extra insurance that she'd have his cooperation. The idea was to disengage his brain while engaging his cock, and she'd noted earlier, with pleasure, that her chosen outfit had indeed done just that. The bulge in Michael's jeans confirmed it more than once, even before she'd made a point of bending to examine sale items set on a low shelf. Oh, but men were so easily entranced, so easily guided. And she knew now that her bare pussy and the twin curves of her ass just peeking from under the tight white fabric of her dress had done the trick with Michael. Plus it just made her feel sexy and like a bad girl; the playful exhibitionist side of her submissive tendencies, she supposed, now helping her steal a skirt.

Her thoughts snapped back to the present. A voice. Michael's.

"Sorry...Mia, was it? Looks like we don't even carry those anymore. I can call the supplier tomorrow, if you want, and see if we can special order them. That could take a few weeks, though. You probably don't want to wait..." He shrugged and turned a key in the register, locking it for the night.

She smiled at him.

"Oh no...Michael. Sorry for the trouble. I just

thought—"

He was still aroused, his erection huge and straining in his jeans, and he was making no effort to hide it now. He'd come around the counter and was looking her up and down, his dark eyes taking in her nipples, the corners of his mouth turning up, approving. His eyes then moved down to her long tanned legs in the black heels.

"Love the white dress."

"Thanks. Look, it's late and I've already kept you from closing up on time. I gotta get going. But thanks again for checking on the fence-net stockings." Her elbow squeezed the shoulder bag in closer to her body as she turned toward the exit. Another rush of satisfaction flooded her. She'd just scored a premium leather miniskirt and was about to walk right out the door with it and leave a hunky guy with a huge hard-on.

"You have a good night, then," she heard his husky voice calling behind her. The red neon of the "open" sign in the front window flickered a little, buzzing, and then went black. Maybe he couldn't wait to get her out of the store. *Probably wants to jerk off.*

Her hand closed around the doorknob when she sensed someone moving up quickly behind her. Before she could turn, a large hand encircled her throat as an arm clamped around her belly, pulling her backward. It happened so fast.

A deep male voice—not Michael's—breathed into her ear.

"Where the fuck do you think you're going?"

✧ ✧ ✧

SHE WENT LIMP. And aphasic. Unable to summon even a fight-or-flight response. Blurry edges of thoughts flashed and then retreated. The hand around her throat allowed her to make a low, garbled noise, but she couldn't scream. This was real; this was happening. She felt a second set of strong arms grab at her arm. The purse was ripped away from her, sent flying.

If they had a knife, she never saw it. Her feet dragged in the high heels, struggling to find solid ground as two men moved her across the floor like an awkward piece of furniture. The pain of their bruising grips kept her gasping, even as instinct for survival told her to yield. A new rush of fear exploded in her as she felt a cold rush of air—the white dress shoved up her thighs, way up. Her bare pussy and ass were exposed and vulnerable.

"Fucking thieving little slut doesn't even bother to wear panties. I've had to watch this cunt for an hour, putting on a show in the front." Michael's voice. His tone told her this wasn't just about the theft of the skirt.

A door swung open, and she was shoved through the threshold and into a dim room she assumed was the stockroom—the same room she'd sent Michael to earlier while she'd swiped the skirt. She stumbled across slick dark tile, tripped in the heels, and fell to her knees. She crawled a few feet to a wall, instinctively, as if cowering near a vertical surface would somehow shield her from them. She looked out at the two men who hovered near her, feeling like a cornered animal. Their leering expressions unnerved her as much as the thought that she was now alone with them and out of range of any help. Who would hear her even if she did scream? Her purse was gone, left in the other room, the cell phone inside it. Her breath came in shallow pants, her chest rising and falling. She dipped her chin, lowering her eyes to look at the dark tile before her, focusing on her breathing, trying to calm herself, to think. She'd try to talk her way out of this.

"Fuck you. You can't prove shit!" she spat, looking up at both men. Fear made her go on the defensive and spew bravado—or at least what she hoped passed for such. What the fuck did they want with her? So she'd swiped a skirt. Big deal. These guys didn't exactly look like they'd walk a grandmother across a busy intersection. Why didn't they just call the cops? She could explain it all. It was a misunderstanding. A big misunderstanding.

The second man's eyes narrowed. "I'd shut up and do as you're told if I were you, you shoplifting slut. You're going to pay for that skirt you stole now. Just not…in cash."

Even in the semidarkness she could see that he was strikingly handsome. Dark shoulder-length hair and a goatee, a muscular lean frame that had to be at least six foot three. His veined forearms were covered with black and gray ink. Both men were fumbling with buttons at the waistbands of their jeans and moving toward her.

Oh God.

Mia squinted, still trying to get her bearings. Her gaze fixed on an object just a few feet from her, centered in the amber of a small spotlight mounted on a crossbeam above it: a heavy polished wooden bench of some kind. Two vertical posts had thick metal cuffs dangling from each just a few inches from the floor. Spanning between the posts, at about waist height, was a black padded surface just wide enough for a human body to be folded over, ass out, bound and helpless. Mia's pulse raced again.

Lengths of rope, whips, canes, and every other kind of kinky implement imaginable were arranged on the dark painted walls and displayed on shelving. All organized, yes, but not packed or boxed or marked for sale. This wasn't inventory. This was a working dungeon. She'd never seen so much kinky equipment in one room. Only in pictures on the internet. This was real. Mia's eyes strained to adjust as a muted golden glow—sconces on the walls—came up slightly.

"Let's get this show going, Cade. I've had a hard-on for this bitch for an hour already." Michael's voice was hard-edged, quiet but strained. "I want her to suck my cock. Now."

"Good idea. I'm gonna handcuff this little whore." Cade's rough grip pulled her to her knees and spun her. She gasped as she felt metal grinding into the flesh of both her wrists, cutting into her skin. Then she heard a clicking sound as the cuffs tightened, binding her wrists together behind her. Pain radiated from her wrists as she tested the metal. No use.

Both men walked around her, predators eyeing their prey before taking it as their own. They stopped in front of her, moving in closer to her face as they unzipped and freed their cocks. A hand reached down and brushed a thick strand of her blonde hair off her cheek, almost tenderly.

"Open. Suck." Michael's voice was calm, but his hard cock shoved past her parted lips and into her mouth. She held still, unsure, hearing the roar of her blood rushing in her ears.

"Don't make me say it again."

She moved her head slowly forward on his hardness, taking his length in, all the way back, as far as she could. As she felt her gag reflex begin, she hesitated, sputtered, felt her cheeks puff as she struggled to accommodate the suffocating fullness invading her mouth. Her eyes watered. His fingers raked a handful of her hair at the base of her neck and twisted hard, pulling her, forcing her to take him over and over at the pace he wanted. Slowly at first. Then faster. Then slower again. She was aware of the other man watching, stroking his cock. She knew he would be next.

"Tongue out. Let me see the tongue, sweetheart. Look at me. Eyes on me."

She looked up. Michael held her on his cock, forcing her head to his groin, keeping her there. The pressure built behind her watering eyes, and she felt a tear spilling down her cheek. She blinked hard but kept her eyes wide, looking up at him, despite the sting of running mascara. In a moment she felt she would pass out if he didn't allow her to breathe. Somehow she managed to move her tongue past her lower lip while he pushed in deeper.

"Ahhh, fuck yes. That's it, girl…" He moaned as his grip tightened again, twisting her hair, controlling her movement, holding her in place on his cock…ten seconds, fifteen, twenty, thirty. He released her with a loud grunt and a jerk. She saw his cock, coated with glistening strings of her saliva, pulling away from her gasping mouth. She realized that the mess—two cocks hard for her attention—was turning her on too.

"I figured she could take a good face fucking, but damn, Cade…" Michael's voice was heavy with lust, admiration.

In the next moment, before she'd been allowed a full breath, Cade fisted a handful of her hair and jerked her head toward his cock, his black jeans bunched just below his groin, the urgency of need for the ministrations of her mouth too much for him to bother with disrobing completely.

"Suck! Go on. Take it down." She knew any protest would be futile. Her wrists strained at her back, locked in the unforgiving steel that cut into her skin. Something about the tone Cade was using, the glint in his eyes, scared her, even as she already felt a betraying wetness between her legs. He stuffed his hard cock into her open mouth and pushed in smoothly. A fresh pool of spit slipped from her lips and ran down her chin as his hardness reached for the back of her throat.

She tried to keep her eyes open and look up at Cade. She saw Michael too, standing just inches away as Cade continued fucking her mouth. He'd stepped out of his jeans and was stroking his cock, watching, breathing. He leaned in suddenly and, with both hands, yanked the fabric that loosely covered her shoulders, pulling her white dress down so her breasts were exposed, vulnerable. He gave one breast a particularly vicious smack; she felt it wobbling back and forth even as her busy mouth, still full of Cade's cock, muffled her own cry at the pain of the blow. Saliva dripped in long strands, forming rivers that ran down her now reddened breasts. The fabric of her dress bunched at her hips. At the small of her back it provided a resting place for her cuffed hands, some small comfort in an otherwise painful and awkward position, kneeling as she was before the two lustful men intent on using her to satisfy their urges.

Michael's husky voice took on a dark, accusing tone. "And what kind of slut comes into my store with a sheer white dress and no bra or panties on, huh?" She felt a sharp, stinging smack on her breast and moaned with Cade's cock still deep in her mouth. Michael punctuated his question with additional staccato slaps at her breasts, some of the slaps landing on her stiffened nipples, making her wince as she sucked cock and tried to keep looking up at Cade. As she'd been told.

Cade fucked her face while Michael continued his rant and slapped at her breasts even harder.

"...bending over every goddamned minute, pretending to look at shit, with your ass sticking out at me? Those fucking hard-ass nipples—" Michael smacked each tit harder again, his other hand still stroking his cock, keeping it ready for her mouth.

Cade pulled free of her mouth with a popping sound, slapping her cheek with his cock. She felt her own slick saliva leaving traces as he rubbed her skin, marking her, claiming her flesh as his to use.

"This little cock slut *likes* being used, I told you. Just look at her messy little face." Cade grunted and yanked Mia's head back, forcing her to look up into his eyes as he spoke.

His tone darkened. "I say we strap this bitch to the bench, cane her, and fuck the shit out of her."

IN HER MIND'S eye she could almost see herself, as if floating just above, looking down at the scene. She could imagine how she must look, bent over the bench, her belly pressing down into the leather padding atop the cross plank, blood rushing to her face, head dropped, wrists and ankles captured inside thick metal cuffs attached to the posts, held motionless almost at floor level. Forced onto her toes by the height of the plank, her calves strained, her ass stuck out. Her bare pussy was exposed and vulnerable. And ready to be caned and fucked by two men.

Cade's voice, behind her again. "Fuck, Mia, you look incredible. I almost hate to do this."

She heard a high-pitched *whoosh* slice through the air behind her. Twice. Three times. Was he warming up his aim, centering? Tormenting? Teasing? The anticipation of the cane had always made her pussy drip. She clenched her ass cheeks in anticipation of impact, in spite of herself. She knew better, yes, but this was different though. Two men forcing this on her…

"Unh unh. No tensing up. Relax your ass or we start over." Michael's command was coming from just above. She opened her eyes slowly and saw his black boots, his lower legs still in his black jeans, which were unzipped but not removed. She felt his cock tapping lightly on her lowered head.

"No dozing, either. Suck my dick." Michael's fist was in her hair again, yanking her head up, forcing his cock at her mouth. Rough. Merciless. His grip tightened, and her scalp burned. He had her attention.

"Open. Wider." She took him in again, and he pushed for the back of her throat. "Yeah, that's it. Take it deep. You love it deep," he rasped, pumping slowly in again. Then all the way out. With each new thrust she struggled to breathe, felt her wrists tensing in the metal cuffs, cuffs that reminded her that she was utterly powerless to do anything about this. She couldn't reach for his cock and use her hands on it, pull it out of her mouth if it was too much. She realized that, if he'd wanted to, he could have held his cock in her throat longer, too long. He would decide when she breathed, how deep she took him. Everything.

At her back, Cade paused, giving her ass a moment to recover from the cane strokes he applied with increasing force. She tried to relax, give in to the inevitable. Accept.

"Five more, I think. Maybe ten. Haven't decided yet. Then I fuck this wet little pussy. Jesus, look at you, dripping. Keep sucking him, Mia. Don't you dare fucking stop. Suck his cock while I cane this ass."

Mia felt her juices beginning to run down the inside of her thigh, while the stripes of fire Cade was giving her ass kept coming. Her strangled yelps were muffled only by Michael's cock.

"And I better not feel even a fucking hint of teeth when he hits your ass with that thing, either." Michael's warning came rumbling at her as he played the head of his thick cock over her lower lip. She breathed while she was allowed to, watching another long string of her drool head toward the floor. She felt his hard length plunge back into her mouth, going deep into her throat, all the way back. Her gag reflex came up again, and it took everything she had to quell it and do as they required.

Don't fight. Relax. You can't do anything about this. They're going to do as they wish.

Michael's guiding fist in her hair kept her speed and depth exactly as he wanted it, while another searing flash of pain erupted on her ass. She kept her mouth open and felt mascara stringing her eyes. She squeezed her eyelids together, hard, concentrating on breathing through the pain Cade was giving her, trying to be open for Michael's cock, an overwhelming confusion of sensations flooded in all at once.

Too much. Too much.

Two rough hands were on her ass now, smoothing over the fleshy cheeks, squeezing gently. She swayed a little—as much as the bench allowed her belly to move at all—under the coolness of Cade's hands, her hips rising a little to meet them, craving their soothing caress, and in the next moment felt Cade's cock at her pussy. He pushed inside slowly through the slick lips of her sex, seating himself deep inside her with a low moan.

The pain of the caning had mostly receded, and she was aware only of Michael's cock, stuffed into her mouth, pumping, and Cade's cock stuffed into her pussy, also pumping. The rhythm sent her into a surreal blissful state, aware of every inch in her pussy and in her mouth.

The continuous motion of both men, the force they exerted on, and into, her body, was making the bench sway a little under her belly. She felt herself rocking between the two of them. Pushed, pulled, but mostly used—as holes for their cocks. Objectified but desired as the center of everything. She allowed herself to let go completely, more than she ever had, and became aware only of the raw sensation as she surrendered to their control. Her delicate wrists and ankles had just enough wiggle room in the heavy metal of the shackles to rub and hurt, reminding her of her predicament, how helpless she was, how utterly at their mercy she was.

And she loved it. She had to admit.

The two men pounded into her relentlessly, their groans deepening as they neared release. She felt Michael's grip tighten on her head, and his cock plunged forward in a powerful thrust. A low moan escaped his lips as his warm seed erupted in spurts in her mouth. She felt him shuddering, holding her on his hardness while Cade pumped in and out of her pussy and smacked her ass, the sting blooming on her plump cheeks.

"Fuck *yes.*" Michael's satisfied growl came from above her as he withdrew his cock from her mouth. She tasted, swallowed, savored the warm saltiness and then watched his lean frame back away slowly from her to shadows. She dropped her head again, all feeling now centered in her pussy as Cade's thick shaft slipped in and out of her slickened sex.

Oh God. I'm going to come.

Cade's thrusts were coming faster, and she knew he was close. His fingers stroked at her swollen clit, and she ground her hips back at him, her orgasm shaking her with rolling deep waves of sensation, making her unable to breathe. When his cock finally slipped out of her, she was surprised, felt the emptiness, the need still there…the loss. But in a moment he was at her face, lifting her head with a rough grip pulling at the nape of her neck, thick fingers twisting in her hair. His cock pressed through her parted lips and into her waiting mouth.

"Open…more…eyes on me now. Good girl."

She did as he demanded and looked up to see his jaw tightening, a strong hand grasping the base of his cock, squeezing, preparing for release.

"Tongue," he rumbled, stroking faster, leaning into her slightly. Her gaze stayed locked into his as she made her tongue wide and flat for him as she waited, her chest heaving, still catching her breath from the pounding she'd taken from both men. She wanted to taste him as much as she wanted to obey him.

With a low groan Cade began to let go, and she felt his warm seed spurting, coating her outstretched tongue, easily overflowing its surface, rolling outward to the corners of her open mouth. Still, she stayed wide open for him, feeling the heaviness of his cock as he tapped her tongue with it. She swallowed, once, twice, and licked her lips as best she could.

Cade pulled away slightly, and her cheek tingled as he stroked it lightly with the back of his hand. She felt him pressing his lips to her forehead.

Michael's deep rumble came from the shadows nearby. "Fuck, Cade, one hell of an idea, I gotta say. I didn't think she'd really go for it."

"Told you she'd love it. She's done nothing but talk about this idea for months. I know how to give my girl what she needs, don't I?" Cade's eyes glittered, crinkling at the corners. Mia smiled up at him.

"Yes, Sir. That was…just amazing." She took in a deep breath and released it, her body going limp over the bench as Cade worked to release her ankles and wrists from the cuffs.

"Happy anniversary, Mia."

This Might Hurt a Bit
Shoshanna Evers

Courtney couldn't help watching the clock. It was almost closing time—almost eleven PM. The little sex shop she'd bought three years ago was practically her whole life, and she had even more work to do when she got home. Somehow she had to dig herself out of the mess she'd gotten into. Her new kinky calendar didn't exist, but she'd sold over a thousand copies of it online—*on preorder*—so yeah, she was officially screwed.

Stupid fucking boyfriend. *Ex*-boyfriend. After everything she'd done for him, to just up and leave her like that? The main reason people went to her website was—unlike most other online sex-toy shops—hers was a high-quality pornographic experience. Enter the site, and not only did customers see the toys, they saw them in action, in all those pics of herself and Travis. No wonder everyone was excited to order her calendar, even if it hadn't been shot yet. Travis was *hot*. She had to give him that. He was also a grade-A asshole for leaving her in the lurch.

How was she supposed to produce her own porn

calendar, completely exclusive to Courtney's Kink Adult Shop, without Travis?

Using stock photos wasn't an option—she had to organize her own shoot to utilize her products and specialty toys. But finding a hot guy willing to do all sorts of kinky things for the camera was not easy out in their truck-stop town in the middle of nowhere. She'd be the woman in the calendar, no problem.

Still, she couldn't afford a professional male model. Her budget to shoot the calendar was, at max, three hundred bucks. Almost all of the money from the preorders had already gone to pay her medical bills from when she spent a month in the hospital with meningitis (and no insurance) two years ago.

What hot guy (other than Travis because he "loved" her, or pretended to so he could use her bank account) was going to pose nude doing naughty things for three hundred bucks? The only men who'd answered her ad on craigslist were not exactly what she'd call appealing.

"Come on," she murmured at the clock under her breath. As if that would make time move faster.

Fuck it. She'd close up early. She made most of her money online anyway. So the real-life customers could suck it for the next half hour.

Courtney got up from her stool behind the counter and stretched, then came around to the front of the shop to do her nightly walk-through. It only took a few moments to make sure the sexy lingerie was all hanging properly, that the costumes were in the appropriate spots, and that none of the sex toys had been messed with.

Everything looked fine, save for a couple of butt plugs that had been put back in the wrong place.

The bell on the front door rang, and she paused, butt plug in hand, and pasted a smile on her face. It was a guy, by himself, (*a really good-looking guy! Wonder of wonders.*) which probably meant he'd go straight to the DVD section with some excuse about a bachelor party, or a gag gift (yeah right). Why did they even have a DVD section anymore, anyways? All the best porn was online; everyone knew that. Hell, some of it was even on her own site.

"Welcome to Courtney's Kink Adult Shop," she said.

The guy nodded, leaning back against the door so it shut all the way. She'd never seen him before—maybe he was from the next town over, or maybe he was on a road trip. *Who knows.* He looked around the shop but kept his black hoodie on his head, his shaggy dark hair falling over one eye.

"You alone here?" he asked.

Instantly her smile faltered. Why the hell did he ask that?

Chill out, Court. Maybe he's just embarrassed.

"We're closing up soon, so let me know if you need help finding something," she said, ignoring his question.

"Who's 'we'?" he asked, stepping closer to her.

He was tall, way taller than she was, and the width

of his shoulders implied that he had some muscles under that hoodie of his.

Courtney's gut instinct was that something wasn't right. Even as her friendly, helpful retail-sales persona tried to combat that feeling, it was too strong to ignore.

She didn't answer his question, and stepped back behind the counter again, closing and locking the little gate that separated the counter from the store. Not that it would stop him from jumping over the damn thing, considering it was only waist-high, but it was a start.

I'm overreacting! No, no I'm not. He's up to something.

Her purse was under the register, and she smiled as she grabbed it and unzipped it, reaching inside. With her fake smile still on her face, she looked at the guy, closing her hand around the cool metal of her gun.

"You know what, man?" she said, keeping her hand on the gun, hidden below the counter. "We're closed. So you should come back another time."

If she wasn't so unnerved, she'd find him really appealing. He looked like he was in his early twenties, maybe, with a handsome face and good teeth, which meant he probably wasn't a meth head or anything. So why was he being so…scary?

Maybe it's just me. Maybe I'm being too paranoid.

"I haven't gotten what I came here for," he said. He didn't smile back at her, which in itself was unnerving.

"What do you need?" She swallowed hard, and hoped he didn't notice he was scaring the shit out of her.

He nodded up to the security camera, which displayed its image on a tiny TV above the register, facing out so customers could see they were being recorded.

"Turn that off," he ordered. He was close now, too close, his body pressed up against the counter, his cool blue eyes staring into hers.

Fuck. Hell no, hell no.

"I can't do that. Get out."

"It wasn't a fuckin' *request*," he said.

She took a shaky breath. "What. Do. You. Want."

If she pulled her gun on him, she'd better be prepared to shoot. Not exactly how she'd envisioned her evening playing out.

The guy reached across the counter and grabbed her wrist—the one attached to the hand holding her hidden gun. His grip was iron on the small bones in her wrist, and she cried out but didn't move.

"Get the fuck off me," she whispered. She'd meant to shout it, but fear took her breath away.

"Goddamn it," he said, and without letting her go, he reached up—close enough so she could catch a whiff of his masculine scent—and turned the camera off. The TV monitor went to static.

Oh God, she'd only bought the stupid gun because she thought having it would be like Murphy's Law—protection against ever needing the damn thing. She didn't want to shoot the kid.

Not a kid. A dangerous man. He was probably less than a decade younger than her, since she had recently turned thirty-three.

But if she pulled the gun out now, she'd have to pull the trigger immediately or he'd just grab it out of her hand. He was bigger and stronger.

"Let me go," she said, forcing herself to sound calm, even as her adrenaline spiked. "And I'll give you all the money in the register, okay? Then you leave."

The guy released her wrist but didn't step back.

"Gimme some space, man," she said.

To her surprise, he stepped back a bit. Interesting.

"My name's Courtney." She wanted to make him see her as a real person, because she'd heard that was good to do.

"I don't want to do this, Courtney," he said. "But I have to. I need the money from the register, but I also need everything you keep in the safe."

"I don't have a safe," she lied.

She *did* have a safe. The store was a million times more secure than her shitty apartment, and she always kept enough cash in the safe to pay all of her expenses for three months, in case the shit hit the fan. Ever since that time her PayPal account had been suspended for selling adult products online—and all the money in her account with them had been frozen—she'd kept cash on hand. Yes, she had a regular bank account, too—half-empty thanks to her shit-bag ex. But cash was king.

How the hell did he know about it, though?

"You have a fucking safe, Courtney. You've got your own store—you've got all this money." He glared at her.

"Yeah, I've seen your fancy website. You don't need that money like I do. So stop lying."

The robber made a move like he was going to grab her again, and Courtney jumped back with her bag, her back pressed against the wall. She was cornered.

"I don't want to shoot you," she said, and finally pulled the gun out of her purse. "But I will. I will fucking shoot you."

His blue eyes widened in surprise. "You're not supposed to have a gun."

Courtney raised her eyebrows. "And yet, I do. Weird, huh. Now get the fuck out of here before I call the cops."

"Look," he said, "please don't call the cops. I…my kid brother got himself into a mess, okay? They're gonna hurt him if they don't get their money. I need it, for him, okay? If I'm in jail I can't help him."

"Should've thought of that before you held me up, asshole."

"Holy fuck." The young man dropped his head into his hands and pushed his hoodie down. "I can't believe this is happening."

"I'm not rich, okay?" Courtney said, the gun still aimed at his chest. "I can't give you money, even if it's for your kid brother. Go get a loan. Pawn shit. Sell your car."

"You don't think I've done all that?" he asked. "I've done everything I could. Everything. This was my last hope." He stared at her gun. "Can you please put that down? I won't hurt you. I just don't want it to go off by accident."

Courtney slowly lowered the gun, keeping her finger outside the trigger guard like she'd been taught. But she wasn't going to drop it or anything. Not until this guy was out of her store.

"What makes you think I have a safe?" she asked.

"I used to work at the place that sold it to you," he mumbled. "Before they canned my ass."

"Smart of them." *Un-fucking-believable.* At least now she knew he was probably from the city. He'd probably chosen her because her store was out of the way of prying eyes.

"I'll leave, okay?" he said finally. "I'm really sorry. I just thought…you've got such a hot fucking website, and the store, and a safe full of cash—"

"Why do you think that? That the safe has money in it?"

He rolled his eyes. "The only reason to keep a safe in a store is to keep money in it, or a gun. I could use either, honestly."

"Well, I've got the gun, so good luck with that. Now get the fuck outta my sight before I shoot you for real."

"Please don't call the cops," he begged. "I'll do anything. Please, Courtney."

"Call me 'ma'am,' asshole. Courtney was my name *before* I had the gun on you."

"Yes, ma'am," he said immediately. "I'm sorry I

tried to rob you—I really am. I'm sorry I scared you. I swear I'll do anything to fix it."

He looked so anguished she almost felt bad for him. Almost.

And then an idea came to her.

"Anything, huh?" she asked.

"Yeah." He looked at her eagerly. "Anything, except give you money, 'cause I've got none. Name it."

"Tell me your name first."

"Fuck. Shane," he whispered.

"Shane what? I'm writing this down in case you skip out on me." She picked up her pen and scrawled his name on the back of one of her store cards.

Are you crazy? Get him out of here! But he was a hot guy, and he was desperate, which meant he actually fit the bill quite perfectly…for the all-new Courtney's Kink Adult Shop Calendar.

"Shane Taylor," he mumbled. He winced when she pulled out her phone and snapped a quick pic of him.

She held her phone for another moment. "That photo and your name just went to my friend. She'll tell the cops if something goes bad, got it?"

He nodded, his entire demeanor changed. No longer the scary criminal, now he looked positively sorry for himself.

"Take off your hoodie, and take off your shirt," she ordered, still keeping her back against the wall.

Shane laughed nervously. "Is this a joke?"

"Not a joke. I thought you said you'd do *anything*."

He stopped laughing. "All right."

"You mean, 'yes, ma'am.'"

He paused, a chagrined expression on his handsome face. "Yes, ma'am."

Slowly, he peeled off his hoodie, letting it drop to the floor by his feet. Underneath, he wore a tight black T-shirt, his heavily tattooed arms now visible.

"Nice tats," she said. She had her whole back done with fairy wings, herself.

"Thanks." He looked at the floor nervously. "You need me to take my shirt off?"

"If you want to," she said.

"And if I don't?"

"Then leave."

He stared at the door for a moment, then shook his head. "You promise you won't call the cops if I stay?"

"Shane," she said, smiling sweetly, "if you do everything I say, not only will I *not* call the cops, but I'll actually *give* you three hundred dollars."

Finally he smiled back at her, his straight white teeth showing. "All right…"

He stripped off his T-shirt, revealing a long, lean, muscled torso with six-pack abs. Perfect.

"Yup, you'll do just fine," Courtney said. "I don't need to hold the gun on you anymore, do I?"

"No, ma'am. I swear."

"Prove it to me. Get naked."

Shane smiled nervously, but he dropped his jeans, kicked off his boots, and finally, with a deep breath, pulled off his boxer briefs.

His cock hung heavy and low, a nice size even if he wasn't hard yet.

"Scared?" Courtney asked, nodding to his cock.

"Yes, ma'am. I'm sorry."

"Well, *I'm not* sorry," she said. "You deserve to be a little scared after that shit you pulled on me."

When he was fully naked, Courtney feigned putting the gun back into her purse. What she really did, with her other hand, was put the gun under a pile of papers by the wastebasket. It was completely hidden, not where he'd expect to find it, and still accessible.

She wasn't sure if that was a smart move, but now that she had him naked and willing to do anything for her, she wasn't afraid of him anymore.

No, if anything, now it was Shane's turn to be scared of *her*.

"So, you've seen my website?" she asked.

"Yes, ma'am. It was hot." Shane glanced at her. "You looked…really good. Fucking sexy as hell."

"Thanks." Courtney shrugged off the compliment, considering who it was coming from, but it did feel good to know she still had it. "Come on, we're going in the back room, where I have everything set up."

Recognition dawned on his handsome face. "You're going to use me for those pics, aren't you."

"Yup." She gestured with her head for him to hurry up and follow her, and he did, like a good little puppy.

She opened the door to her back room, complete

with her specialty bondage bed and chair, and the lights on metal stands, all in place, ready to go. Courtney flipped on the lights, and the room was illuminated perfectly. Along the back, sturdy shelves housed boxes of products, ready to ship.

"Holy shit," he breathed, taking it all in. "But if you're in the photos, who takes the pics?"

Courtney pointed to her three high-resolution video cameras, each set up to capture a different angle of the scene.

"When I was still with Travis, we just filmed ourselves having fun with the toys, and took stills from the shots."

Shane whistled. "You've got videos of that stuff? Why don't you just make a porno and sell it?"

"It's something to think about," she murmured.

The truth was, in pictures she could take her time to Photoshop them, make everything look awesome, and pick and choose the best angles and most flattering shots. She'd watched her videos, and professional adult films they were *not*. The photo stills that came out of them, though? Perfection (at least, once she'd edited them a bit).

"Now," she said, turning the cameras on, "if you need me to stop doing something, or if I need you to stop, we'll use a safe word. What's your safeword?"

"I…I don't have one."

"I'll give you one. Let's have 'Call the cops' be your safeword, how about that?" She smiled wryly. Fuck him and his criminal ass.

"Yes, ma'am," he mumbled.

"And mine will be me shouting 'fire.' Got it? Keep going after I say 'fire,' and you officially turn into a rapist scumbag, okay?"

His eyes widened. "I'd never do something like that. I swear."

"Well, it's not like I can trust you, now is it?"

She stripped her clothes off, all business, and shimmied into a lacy black negligee. When she turned back to look at him, his cock had gone from limp to hard, jutting out obscenely.

"You should still be scared, by the way," she added, nodding at his erection.

"Okay." He smiled, his fears clearly gone at the sight of her scantily-clad body.

Courtney sighed and pushed him onto the bed. His chest was hard-packed muscle beneath her hands.

"We're going to play with some new toys. First up, this sex ramp." She pulled the large black ramp onto the bed. "Lie down on your stomach, ass in the air."

"Aww, fuck me," he groaned.

"Later…if you're good."

He sprawled on top of the ramp, and she quickly checked each of the cameras to make sure they were still in alignment from the last shoot.

"I'm going to use these fabric cuffs on you," she said, opening up a pair from her new shipment. "They go with the ramp."

He nodded, and she latched his hands to the sides of the ramp, securing the thick Velcro, and added two larger cuffs for his muscular thighs.

"How's it feel?" she asked, admiring the view. Damn, he looked good like that, all restrained and at her mercy.

"I'm not safewording," he said.

"Good. Now let's introduce the purple leather flogger. I'm going to make your ass nice, red, and stripy for this scene," she said, bringing it out.

The flogger was good quality but not too expensive—something her customers would love, especially after seeing pics of her applying it to Shane's butt.

"Wait—you're going to make my ass red with makeup, right?" Shane looked back at her with an expression of concern mixed with arousal.

Yes, definitely arousal. That was gonna make a nice pic, right there.

Courtney laughed. "No makeup, buddy. In fact…this might hurt a bit."

He took a deep breath. "Yes, ma'am. I suppose I deserve it, anyway. I never should have tried to rob you. I'm really sorry."

"Nice. Trying to get me to go easy on you. I can respect that." Courtney grinned and circled the bed, flinging the flogger through the air to catch a few shots of it with the strands all flying. "But it won't work."

Shane shut his eyes. "Oh my God, please, just do it already."

"As you wish." The flogger sliced through the air with a satisfying sound and landed directly on his ass, leaving behind beautiful red lash marks.

"Oww!" he cried.

"Oh come on, this is a *baby* whip. Seriously. Don't be a pussy."

"I'm okay," he said.

"This one's for holding me up, asshole." She flogged him again, harder, and he stifled his moan against the ramp.

Curious, Courtney leaned over the bed and felt between Shane's young, hard body and the ramp. His cock was at full mast despite his whining. She'd whipped herself with the very same flogger when it first came in stock, so she knew it was perfect for kinky beginners.

She flogged him again a few more times, just enough to get his ass the perfect color (and, truth be told, to appease her need for a little painful vengeance). Shane cried out with each lash, his face flushed.

He moaned and shifted his weight against the ramp, then did it again. And again.

"Stop trying to cheat yourself to an orgasm, mister," she warned.

He paused. "Sorry, ma'am."

She dropped the flogger on the bed. "Next up, the prostate stimulator for men." She took the long, thin vibrator with the tiny egg-shaped head over to the front of the ramp so Shane could see it for himself.

"That sounds like you want to put that in my ass," he said.

"I do." She turned it on, touching the vibrating tip with her finger. Felt good!

"Nothing goes up my ass," Shane said, full of bravado. "Ever."

"Shane, if this is a hard limit for you, I'll respect that. Just say your safe word."

He shook his head. "I can't do that."

Courtney sat down by his head and stroked his shaggy black hair. He peered up at her with those cool blue eyes of his. But they weren't so cool now, were they? The emotion emanating from his gaze melted her resolve.

He was aroused, but she could see he was a bit frightened, too…of what she might do to him. Now that he wasn't robbing her, scaring the shit out of her, she held the reins. But…this wasn't right.

It didn't *feel* right, not anymore.

She didn't want to feel weird about this whole thing. Yeah, he was a fuckup, but if he deserved anything, it was to go to jail for trying to rob her store, not to get ass-fucked by a sex toy instead.

Fuck. Why did her conscience have to come into play right now, right when she thought she had it all figured out?

"I'm sorry, Shane. I was…it was wrong of me to put you in this situation."

She unlatched his cuffs, and he rolled over, naked,

onto the bed—wincing slightly as his freshly-whipped ass made contact with the sheets.

"Wait—what's going on?"

"I'm feeling a little weird and rapey right now," she said, shrugging as if it didn't matter. But it did. "So just leave, okay? I'm letting you go."

She expected the next words out of his mouth to be another request that she not call the cops, but he said nothing. Just stared at her.

"Lemme see that," he said, taking the toy from her hand. "What's it feel like?"

"Um…well, it's gotten great reviews on other sites," she said. "Supposed to give you an amazing orgasm in seconds."

He smiled at her. "You know, I could use that three hundred bucks. Let's give this a shot."

Courtney laughed, shaking her head. "I was taking advantage of you because you held me up. You're worth more than three hundred bucks for a shoot like this, you know? But I don't have any more to give, because the money for my calendar is already gone. Spent. I'm in the hole right now, and just struggling to get out of it."

"Kinda like me," he said.

"Yeah. Kinda like you." She sighed and flopped back on the bed next to him.

"I don't care," he said suddenly. "Let's do it. I could use an amazing orgasm."

"Really?"

"Yeah." He started to lie back on the sex ramp, but

Courtney stopped him and pushed the ramp off the bed. It landed with a soft *whomp* on the floor, out of sight.

"All right, let's do this," she whispered. She raised her voice, relishing the desire written all over Shane's face. "On your hands and knees, center of the bed, facing the camera so we can catch your expression."

Shane laughed and did as he was told. "Anyone ever tell you you'd make a hell of a dominatrix?"

"All the time."

She lubed up the toy and slowly, ever so carefully, inserted it inside him, watching his face, listening to the beautiful groans and moans he made when she turned the vibrator on.

"Oh my God, oh my God," he cried. He came hard, his muscles tensing, standing out in stark relief, then relaxing completely. He fell over onto his side and looked up at her. "Wow. Just...wow."

"It's gonna be a huge seller," she said in agreement.

"What else you got for me?" he asked, smiling in his postorgasmic haze. "I'm yours."

"What about helping your kid brother?"

"Actually...it's me who got into trouble. Gambling debts from a couple years ago. Stupid shit. I don't do it anymore—I learned my lesson." He paused. "I know you said the money for the calendar is already gone, but what if we worked something else out?"

Hmm. "If you'll be my new model, I can give you a portion of the proceeds for future sales I make using your image," she said.

Hell, that was better than having her mooching ex-boyfriend just take what he wanted from her bank account all the time. And it felt a lot more fair, too.

"I could use that income to pay off my debts," Shane said, nodding. "And…it'll give me a chance to try and make things up to you." He stuck out his hand. "It's a deal."

Courtney grinned and shook his warm hand, relishing the feel of his smooth skin against her palm. "This…this could be good. I'm almost glad you robbed me tonight, Shane."

Their faces were just millimeters apart, his naked body next to hers on the bed arousing something deep and primal within her. Lust.

"…really?" he asked.

"It probably would have been better if you'd just asked me out instead," she amended.

Damn, he was cute. And if he'd asked her out, she wouldn't have had an excuse to whip his perfectly-muscled ass, right?

"Can I ask you out now?" he asked. His lips were so close…

"Don't push it."

She didn't mean to, but those lips—how could she resist? "You've probably still got some punishment coming to you," she warned, and dropped a quick kiss to his lips.

He responded so eagerly, so sweetly, that before she

knew it, the moment intensified, their tongues dancing together. They kissed with the awe and reverence only a new lover's kiss can ignite.

She pulled away reluctantly. "Before we go on, I need to finish closing up the store, and put away my gun."

"Thanks for not shooting me, by the way," he said.

Courtney nodded. "Thanks for making it up to me. But no more robbing people, okay? You're a porn model now."

"Mama will be so proud." Shane winked, and she couldn't help but to wink back.

Her evening had turned out way better than she ever could have imagined.

Want more from Shoshanna Evers? You can read the BECOMING HERS TRILOGY SET, an erotic female dome/male sub romance.

The Bombshell
Candy Quinn

THE VISITOR'S CENTER of the prison was always a noisy place. Families came to visit, women, men, kids, lots of tears, some yelling, a few laughs even. It was a big open area where the guards watched from the sidelines, rarely needing to intervene but always a constant reminder of the fact that the men were still prisoners, even as they got a sampling of the outside world.

There was only one visitor who came to visit Sean Flaherty anymore. The woman he had met through correspondence was nothing he had expected. Years of being locked up and without visitors had left him desperate for any outside contact, and he was prepared to be grateful for most any woman who wished to visit him.

Yet every time she walked through that door...the only word that came to mind was *bombshell*.

Years of being an inmate had left him a lot of time to hone his body to its physical peak, but he had little access to anything else that might improve his looks. His dark hair was kept trimmed at least, but without proper grooming tools he had opted to shave his old beard right off.

Still, every time she saw him, her face lit up. As if it were she that was grateful and impressed by him. Somehow.

She wasn't just pretty, with sweet girl-next-door eyes and a trim waist. How could she be, when she also had such surreal breasts and a perfectly sculpted ass? Her mouth was done up with a delicious pink lipstick, and her eyelashes made her look more innocent than he knew her to be.

She'd written him so many letters. So many filthy, tempting letters.

Her hair fell in large, loose waves and perfectly framed her face as if she was just walking out of a magazine spread. Each step of her long, toned legs made his cock stiffen in anticipation, her skirt shrinking up her thighs.

But when she leaned in, and her hair tickled his face, and he smelled the coconut perfume and saw down her shirt...

It was so many little, subtle things, and as her lips brushed against his ear, he almost felt like it was too much. The scent of her surrounding him, the way her white blouse formed a V along her cleavage just right, the fact that he could see that black lace bra beneath.

Vivian was too good to be true.

His fists had clenched without him realizing, and he had to force himself to relax, to tone back those powerful urges as he brought his large, tough hand to hers. Her slender digits so dainty and delightful, with beautifully made-up nails. He gave that hand a tight squeeze in his powerful grasp, and his gravelly, harsh voice rumbled out to her.

"So fuckin' good to see you again, Viv." He wanted to toss her onto the table between them and fuck her then and there. Lord knows the many jealous eyes on them were thinking much the same, he told himself.

Her smile broadened as she pulled back slightly, her deep blue eyes staring into his. "I've missed you." She sounded so goddamned genuine! He couldn't imagine a girl like her being hard up for dates outside these walls, but then…he knew her fantasies. Her desire for a real "bad boy," not one of those pampered rich dudes who owned a bike and thought they were badass.

Locked away for murder as Sean was, that definitely meant he qualified.

He tugged her arm in a harsh grasp, and he lifted her hand, placing a kiss on her delicate fingers. His hard, emerald eyes stared into her blue gaze. "Damn it, Viv," he muttered, such suppressed emotions rumbling beneath the surface. "You got no idea what it takes to resist throwing you on this table, yankin' that little slutty skirt of yours up and takin' a crack at that sweet cunt of yours right here and now."

It would've been simple dirty talk for most couples, but as he rubbed her fingers over the dark stubble of his jawline, she knew it wasn't.

A shiver of excitement went through her, and even the lacy bra couldn't hide the stiffening of her nipples beneath the light material. She definitely didn't use, or need, any padding.

She lingered so very near to him, letting her sweet scent surround him before she swallowed and sat on the bench next to him. Her legs crossed, her ankle rubbing against the harsh material of his pants.

"I couldn't sleep last night," she murmured, looking so damned shy and submissive. He knew she wasn't. She was a manager or something at one of the local offices, and she did all their PR. No shy girl could do that, especially not at her age. She was only thirty, after all.

"I just kept thinking of seeing you." Her hand fell to his thigh, squeezing it in her manicured grasp, feeling the hard, corded muscle beneath. Not an inch of his physique was without the sculpted toning he worked so hard on.

More prominent even than the bulge of that muscle was the heat of his loins, his cock so damn stiff in his pants as he sat beside her.

Sean reached up, cupped her soft, smooth cheek and stroked his thumb across her beautiful face. "Won't be long now," he muttered to her, barely restraining himself. In fact, it was only the truth of that statement that kept him in check at all. "If it wasn't for that, I'd say to hell with these fuckers and pounce you right now, Viv," he said, wetting his lips. "I'd say to hell with good behavior, and just make the most of this time in the way that matters."

He narrowed his eyes with such longing. "Fuck, you are one perfect beauty."

She flushed as if she'd never heard that before. Her cheeks turned rosy, and her breasts swelled with her quickened breath. "I can't wait to get you home," she whispered back into his ear, her voluminous hair blocking her lips from any spying guards. "To see what you're capable of."

He grabbed her thigh abruptly with his free hand, with a strong, hard grasp that immediately wedged its way between her shapely thighs. He didn't do it gently, but he brought his hand up to her sex there in the middle of the room, surrounded by dozens of other inmates and their families. "You're a good girl," he growled, feeling the bare flesh of her puffy slit, no panties in the way to prevent his touching her. "But you might regret that by the time I'm finished riding you." The dark words were filled with both promise and threat as he grinned at her with such an uneven, dark expression.

Her head tilted back, her light brown hair cascading over her back as she arched her breasts toward him. Oh, how badly did she want that! It was all she could talk about in her letters.

Though in person there was another topic she loved hearing about. She was too bright to write about it, to try to tempt him to incriminate himself further. But she loved hearing about why he was there. About what he'd done.

"I can handle it," she promised.

His grin curved higher across one cheek as he brushed his hand back into her thick, luscious head of hair. He couldn't help but adore those soft waves. "You better be," he nearly growled, rubbing his thick, strong fingers against her bare little slit, prying those labia apart to finger her clit.

It wasn't fair, after all, that she got to torture him so while he was in prison, unable to do anything about it, without torturing her in return.

"You know I don't like to see beauty wasted," he murmured, a reminder of what he had done in such a twisted manner. "And yours is too precious to want to see wasted on the first night out of here."

Her breath was so quick, and she rubbed her button nose along his jaw, along the cusp of his ear. Her body was screaming for him, and she parted her legs as she invited his cruel torture. "I'll last."

Getting carried away, he couldn't help but slide a finger inside of her narrow little cunt, let his thumb rub her sensitive nub of a clit and imagine what it was going to feel like to finally get his dick into her after so long. His lips found hers, and he kissed her in a wet, messy, passionate embrace. He delved his tongue into her mouth, searching out her moist muscle as they made out then and there amid the throng of people.

Those sweet moments of tasting her mouth, her pinkened lips, and inhaling her rich feminine scent were almost too much for him. His thickly corded muscles twitched as he nearly pushed her back onto the table before a guard called out. "Flaherty!"

All the same, he was slow to break it off and gave her lips a few more sensuous kisses, their mouths smacking moistly as he slipped back and stared into her eyes. He retreated his hand and circled her clit as the guard went away, satisfied that they weren't too obvious about their violations of the rules.

He'd left her breathless, and her blue eyes were heavy with arousal. She'd been so close. So, goddamned close to making a mess all over the prison bench. Just a few threatening words of warning, his fingers working her clit, and she was all his.

"Not long," she whimpered. "It's all set up."

Sean licked around his lips, tasting the fleeting remnants of their kiss as he squeezed her soft inner thigh and gave her one last teasing swirl of his finger. "Good," he said in a grunt. "Won't be long then, and I'll have you all to myself, Viv. I'll be out of here for good, and you'll be mine. All mine."

The guard returned and tapped his baton against the wall beneath the clock. "Wrap it up, Flaherty," he told Sean in a dry voice.

"Where's the time go, huh?" Sean remarked and then shamelessly shoved his mouth to hers again, bending her back as he held her in his thick, muscled arms. He kissed her so deep, making such a lewd display of it in the middle of the room as he said his good-bye.

"Damn it, Flaherty!" complained the guard as he stomped toward them.

It wasn't until the guard grabbed hold of his shoulders and yanked him back—twice!—that he pulled away from her and got up.

"Don't fuck it up," he told her. "I'm countin' on you."

Her face was so pink with her arousal that she seemed in a daze, but still she nodded obediently. "I won't. I'll see you soon" She smiled up at him, letting him stare down at her pillowy breasts. "Be good."

He made no effort to hide the obvious bulge in his pants as he strode away, grinning with satisfaction. Knowing what was to come.

✧ ✧ ✧

BEING IN JAIL for murder meant there was no real hope of getting out. He was still a decade off from any option of parole even. It was the kind of thing that would've driven him mad if he didn't know what awaited him. That freedom would be his soon, regardless if the parole board wanted it to be so or not.

He lay on his prison bed, resting his hand on his thick forearms as he waited and thought. He'd napped and was ready to go, blood coursing through him with anticipation.

The slow, steady footsteps of the guard resounded before stopping by his cell.

Without a word Sean got up and stood before the

door.

It was the same guard who had hauled him away from Vivian, and Sean gave him a simple stare nodding. The door slid open, and they quietly strode away.

The prison was dead quiet at night, and Sean did his best not to disturb it any more than necessary. It wasn't until they had gotten to the guard offices that either of them spoke.

"You really need to make that fuckin' scene in the visitation hall?" complained the guard.

"Ah, it works for the best anyhow, Rufus. Makes it look like I ain't thinkin' I'll get out anytime soon. Besides," he said as he began to strip off his prisoner's garb and change into the simple gray uniform of a prison maintenance staff worker "could you blame me? You saw that fine piece of ass I got," he remarked with a self-satisfied grin.

"Fair enough," admitted Rufus reluctantly, taking the discarded clothes and stuffing them into a garbage bag, which he handed Sean as he finished dressing.

Tugging the cap onto his head, Sean followed after Rufus. The prison was quiet, and there weren't many guards on staff at night. Though a few of them were passed, none paid the two any mind. They looked perfectly in place, after all.

Through the labyrinthine corridors they at last came to a back exit, and the cool night air struck Sean like the first feeling of freedom.

"Over here," Rufus directed him to a nearby delivery

truck. It was simple, plain and white. "Hop in. I'll drive you outside the gates to the drop-off point," he instructed.

As Sean climbed in back and settled into the darkness once again, he tried to distract himself from thoughts of Vivian. Thinking on her would do more than distract him, he knew. Such a fine woman served only to cloud his judgment.

No, instead he thought on how remarkable it was that she had gotten everything to fall into place. Sure, he had found out about Rufus's predicament, the old guard needing a big dose of cash to sort out some medical bills, but it was Viv who got together the quarter million, made the plan to their mutual satisfaction.

Sean felt the truck lurch out of the prison yard and began its journey.

The trip wouldn't be too long, he knew, and it wasn't even half an hour before the truck pulled to a halt off on a dirt path beside the road.

Up rolled the back door, and Sean stepped out to true freedom at last, seeing the beautiful car parked nearby and knowing it could only belong to one person. The side door opened and Vivian stepped out, though she was just a dark silhouette to him then.

Sean ran to her and scooped her up in his powerful arms. "You did it, babe," he growled victoriously.

She was dressed more covertly than he was used to, despite the ostentatious vehicle. Her black skirt, a black blouse, black tights... Thigh-highs, he hoped. He didn't know if he could stand the extra moment's pause, not at this point.

She wrapped her arms around his neck, drawing him into her, feeling him out as her legs encircled his waist. "We can't linger here," she reminded him, but her lips were already on his neck.

Sean groaned, feeling his manhood stiffen and that deep clouding of his judgment setting in already. She did such wicked, wonderful things to him.

He squeezed her tight, then at last managed to pry her off him and place her back down. There was still something left to do.

Rufus put his phone away. "My wife says she found the money in the drop-off point, just as you said in the call." The remark was directed at Vivian, but Sean was the one who strode over to the man and replied.

"Then that just leaves one last thing." The two men stared at one another, a moment of tense silence. Then Sean struck out, his iron-hard fists impacting the older man's stomach, then belting him across the jaw.

Rufus's graying hair was disheveled as he jerked with the blows before Sean shoved the man into the back of the truck. "Jesus!" Rufus cried out in shock, spitting blood onto the floor of the vehicle.

"Gotta make it realistic, or else what's the point?" Sean said with a wicked sneer before climbing up in back of the truck and dragging the man to the end, where he laid into Rufus some more. The impacts of fists on flesh sounded like he was tenderizing a great slab of meat.

By the time he climbed out of the back, Rufus was little more than that. Barely breathing, the guard was left unconscious as Sean returned to Vivian, grabbed her around the waist, tugged her to him and put his blood-spattered hand back between her thighs as he kissed her fiercely. The blood pumping through him was spurred on by both violence and desire.

And with her, it was no less than that. He'd never felt her so ravenous, and he knew she wouldn't stop him. Stop anything.

No matter how dangerous it was, she was putty in his hands at that display of power. Of control.

Of rage.

Time was of the essence; their whole scheme—his life, his freedom!—depended on them getting on with their plan. Yet the vigorous pumping of his heart surged blood to his muscles. He grabbed her and pinned her against the side of the car. He squeezed her outer thighs as he shoved her black skirt up.

His mouth left hers, and he kissed across her face and back to her neck, where he bit her, grinding the thick, throbbing bulge of his manhood betwixt her legs, all the while breathing out a huff of ravenous, bestial desire.

Her moan was so fucking sweet. Never had he met a woman like Vivian. Never had he known such a woman existed, because the way she ground against him only spoke to one thing: he'd made her intensely wet pummeling that man.

He could feel it, even, between her thighs. Her slick cunny was so inviting, so fucking tempting despite the risk. Blissfully, she was wearing thigh-highs and no panties, nor a bra. She was scandalously bare beneath her dark outfit.

"Fuck," she moaned, grinding against his hand, her ass pressed to the door of her car.

They wouldn't have the whole night before the actual maintenance workers found the truck gone and notified the guards. Yet he couldn't control himself, not with her. Certainly not after so long without. Only her filthy letters that, instead of sating his desire, spurred it on and kindled it higher.

He pushed his hand under her blouse, grasped her breast and squeezed it tight, let that heavy mound of tit flesh meld to his grasp supplely, her body so glorious. Matured to perfection, he thought as he took his other hand from her thigh and began to undo his borrowed pants.

He had to have her. Then and there.

His thick, throbbing organ sprang free. No smaller than he had promised her in his letters, it was ribbed with bulging veins and coursing full of hot blood that made it strain and ache in the cool night air.

He rocked his hips, jabbing his masculine girth at her slick little slit. No slow buildup, no easing it in, just thrusting his hips until he landed it on target and pushed deep into her slick, moist cunt. A loud, noisy groan of satisfaction broke the seal of his mouth on her neck as that first touch of a woman's quim after so many years felt better than he ever remembered or imagined.

And she was so tight! He swore she hadn't been with another man in just as long, though he had no idea how that could be true. This sweet, sweet pussy was just begging for a pounding.

But then, who else could fuel her desires like him?

She bit his neck, lapping over it with her tongue before moving up to his ear, tugging on it with her teeth. Her voice was breathy, wanton in the chill night air. "Tell me about it. About what you did."

"You sick fuck," he growled, but her depravity only excited and pleased him more. His dick swelled within her, and he wasted no time tugging back his hips and then thrusting in, pumping her sweet little cunt up against the side of the car.

His rough voice grew lower as he grunted and moaned, but he obliged her. Was happy to. "She wanted it, and I gave it. I pounded her cunt the whole night through, but that little bitch wailed and cried for me to stop by the end." He huffed as the whole car rocked, the crash of his hips striking her loins adding a wet slap to the cacophony of creaking and groaning.

"Oh God," she moaned, her head tilting back and her pussy squeezing him tighter, rewarding him for his story and begging for more at the same time. She shivered all around him, her muscles and nerves so excited as he fucked her. She felt so unreal, and her fingers ran to his hair, scratching his scalp as she groaned for him.

It had been so long, and she was so tight he knew he couldn't last forever, especially not with the hard, fast fucking he was giving her in his desperate state. The swing of his heavy balls slapped against her ass as he took her with such a crushing hold.

"She whimpered and sobbed and said she'd call the cops on me." He grunted, feeling the twitch in his loins as the fire built from his sac and grew higher. "She couldn't take it." He bit her earlobe hard before letting it snap back. "I wrapped my hands around her slender little neck, and…and"—he began to shake, his balls tightening against him as his climax approached and overtook him before he could finish his sentence.

"I can take it," she whimpered, and he knew she believed it. Especially as she began to shudder, her body trembling in the way that only a woman's body could. Only when it had been driven to such heights of pleasure.

Her body jerked and spasmed, and her breath hitched in her throat as she climaxed as well.

Perfect timing, was the only thought he could conjure up as he shot his load right into her. So much of his thick, virile seed spraying into the wave of hot honey that washed over his aching dick. Such a beautiful mixture of sensations, like no other he'd experienced.

Sean shot every drop of spunk he had in him into that tight snatch, battering her puffy little labia with the final thrusts as his ass clenched and he roared the finale of his pleasure.

His loins spent then he rested against her, panting and huffing.

And this was only the start. A promise for the future.

She huffed against him, and her sweet whimpers of after currents running through her were delightful. It was many moments before she finally whispered, "I have a place they'll never find you. You can hide there until things blow over and we can get away together."

That stiff shaft of his twitched inside her, and she could feel he was already prepared to go again, but he mustered enough control to pull out and let her down, the thick, pearly white essence of his dribbling out of the puffy folds of her well-fucked cunt.

"C'mon then," he growled, pulling open the car door and guiding her in. "I'll drive; you tell me the way."

His command sent another tendril of pleasure through her spine, and she smiled. "Yes, sir."

✧ ✧ ✧

MORNING WAS STILL another hour or so off by the time they pulled up to her place. A beautiful large home away from the city itself. She hadn't been lying about her swanky, high-paying job; there were no doubts about that. She'd paid the bribe to get him out, owned a beautiful expensive car and lived in a home that was easily ten times the size of any place he'd ever lived.

With a sharp whistle he put his arm around her and tugged her close as he leaned in and suckled her ear. "Place this big. It's no wonder you got a nice hidey-hole for me in there somewhere. The cops would get lost searching the place," he said with a broad grin, pushing open the door.

"You don't know the half of it," she purred, and it seemed to him that she was more alive than ever. Even though it'd been a long night, she looked excited, and her eyes flashed at him. "You'll have to lay low for a while, but then"—her grin broadened—"then there will be something even better."

His broad, chiseled jaw spread in a toothy grin as he got out with her. The trees rustled in the breeze around her place as they headed inside.

"I've got lots of supplies down there for you," she explained as she showed him through the place. "And I'll spend all the spare time down there with you I can," she admitted with a flush of her cheeks, another sign of that continued arousal.

"Damn right you will." He grinned, putting his arm around her, his large hand on her hip as he held her close through the journey.

"And once things blow over, then we can slip off in the night together to live on a beautiful beach somewhere." She gave him a bright smile.

Sean Flaherty had no idea how he'd gotten so lucky, but after all he'd been through, he felt he deserved such a break. "Damn, that does sound nice," he growled as she took him down into the cellar.

It was a nicely kept spot but seemed to be home to little more than tools and a wine rack. It wasn't until she went to one of the walls and unlocked a hidden latch that she tugged open a secret door that led farther down.

He whistled. "Damn. How'd you get this all set up in secret anyhow?" He looked her over. That buxom beauty did not look like the handy sort, after all.

"Was here when I got the place." Excitement shone in her eyes as her tongue licked around her full, plush lips, leaving them glossy. "It's practically ancient. An old root cellar, I guess," she explained as she went down the old stairs.

Down below he could see just how old the place was, but it had everything he needed. A big bed, TV, computer, a bunch of boxed supplies, and even some weights for him to work out with.

"You really did get it all set up just for me," he remarked with a satisfied grin, grasping her hips and tugging her body back against his.

"Of course!" Again he felt that excitement she had for him, and her mouth sought his. She pushed her tongue into his mouth with abandon, and her hands worked their way over his hard muscles. "I need you."

She was full of desire for him, so perky and gorgeous. The perfect woman.

✧ ✧ ✧

HE GRASPED HER tight and knew he'd have to hold on to her for a nice long while as the two of them stripped away his clothes. Got those workman's trousers off of him, his thick thigh and calf muscles exposed. Then came the shirt and tank beneath, exposing the hard ridges of his well-defined abs, bulging pecs and rock-solid biceps.

In return he simply tore open her blouse, popping off more than a couple of buttons as he grabbed her and lunged his mouth for her breast, his greedy mouth sucked a teat in.

God, it felt good, having her soft, supple flesh surround his lips as he drew out that hard nipple. She was horny for him. His dream woman, and she was even more desirous for him. He didn't question how or why, and she moaned with such a pleasant, throaty sound.

Questioning such a beautiful turn of fortune would be madness. Instead he simply satisfied himself with suckling her big, beautiful tit. Flicking his tongue over the stiff pink nub. Making her moan and whimper with his hard affection until he had his fill and pushed her onto the bed.

He slid away those formfitting boxer briefs next, showing his big, meaty cock as he pounced over her on the bed.

"You need me." He repeated her words back to her as he grasped her shoulders and looked over her form before him. Her splayed legs, her exposed breasts with the one nipple and areola glistening wet with his saliva.

"You got me, babe," he declared, groping along her thighs, tugging her skirt up until it was barely more than a belt about her waist.

A body made for sin. She was gorgeous. She should be a model or something, not some executive. She'd shaved her pussy for him, and it was so swollen with arousal. The outer labia swallowed its smaller petals, leaving her so clean and delicate looking but for the slickness that marred her.

"I can take it," she pleaded with him.

He grinned at her eagerness to put herself to that test. Even though he didn't want to break her—not yet, anyway—her words prodded him on, and he couldn't help but take hold of those hips of hers and line up his bulging cock, with that prominent crown, along her slit.

"We'll see," he remarked with a smug grin, digging his thumbs into her so hard as he held her in place that she'd undoubtedly bruise. In one swift motion, he stabbed his massive girth into her like a dagger, impacting deep inside her as he hilted. The noises of his grunts and the squelching of his dick with her honey and his come from his last orgasm filled the room as he began to pump into her.

There was no easing into it again; he'd been without so long, and she was begging for it. Begging for it! Such an eager bitch, he marveled inwardly as he built up his pace, that hard ass of his clenched as he bucked his hips.

Despite the fact that she knew what had happened to the last girl. The last person who had tested her ability to take it, to keep him satiated.

She'd pleaded with him for the story, for every gory last detail. She'd wanted to hear it, and it only made her hornier.

Vivian was sick, and he loved that about her.

Her legs wrapped around his ass, and she drew him in. "Tell me again!"

Thirty years old, successful, more gorgeous than any woman had a right to be, and perverted to the core. Sean couldn't help but grin in rapturous delight at his good fortune as he rewarded her depravity with a harder stab of his cock, slamming his crown against her cervix with each jarring impact.

"You wanna hear about how I fucked that little bitch's womb open?" he said between grunts, the slap of his balls against her ass growing louder and louder. "How I smacked her pretty lil' face around to get her to stop crying? Or just how I choked her with my bare hands while I was still inside her little twat?"

The questions were teasing, giving her some of what she wanted while being such a controlling prick about it.

"All of it!" she pleaded and begged, her legs taut around his ass, her body arching and writhing beneath him. He was driving her crazy with his own sick perversions. Though really, she'd brought it out of him. Moved him past any negative feelings, any shame, any regret, and just turned his horrific past into arousal.

Pure, disturbing arousal.

He couldn't help but moan, his cock swelling within

her, forcing her narrow little canal out wide as he plunged into her and yanked out with the strong, smooth motions of his well-defined hips and ass, her heels digging into his buttocks as he continued his merciless pace.

With one hand he grasped one of her breasts, clenched that fleshy, supple mound. With the other he reached up and slid his powerful fingers around her neck slowly. "Or do you just wanna feel what it's like personally?" he said in a dark, ominous voice.

He bent over her, his fingers tightening around her neck, choking off her breath almost entirely. "She wasn't even the first, y'know." His confession was punctuated by the slick noises of cock sliding along puffy, tight folds, honey-soaked balls striking her fleshy ass.

Her eyes widened, but with glee. With excitement, and even though she could barely breathe, she nodded. Encouraged his story.

"They never found out about the other," he confessed with sick pleasure, angling his hips so he jabbed his steel-hard weapon of a dick into her, causing her free tit to jiggle and sway with the jarring impact.

He bit his lower lip to suppress the deep, loud moan his body insisted on emitting, muffling the sound before he continued. "She was such a tight little treat too. Much like you, my sweet pet," he said in such a growling voice, moving his thumb up over her cheek even as he continued to choke off her air.

He could see the panic begin to play behind her eyes, behind her excitement, and knew that only added to her pleasure. This was what she wanted, wasn't it? He'd read about it in one of the psychology books, about people who craved fear and pain. They needed it, like he needed to give women those things.

His lover's deep satisfaction was echoed back in him, and his eyes rolled back into his head. His manhood twitched, and his scrotum tightened up beneath his ass.

Such a loud, rumbling roar of satisfaction traveled up out of his broad chest, and he hammered out another spine-tingling climax, the thick rivulets of come shooting up against her cervix, coating her insides and adding to the last explosive unleashing as he loosed all he had.

It wasn't until he was done that he softened his grip and let her breathe again, to fall atop her voluptuous form and pant.

He wasn't sure how many hours had gone by, filled with dark pleasures. At some point he must have passed out, though, as there was no way he remembered the feeling of tight pressure around his bare wrists and ankles.

Cold steel cut into him, and he opened his eyes groggily to stare at his bombshell with a Taser pointed right at his chest.

The cold smirk told him all he needed to know. She elaborated anyways.

"You're mine now," she purred in that once-sensuous voice, "and you've got two women's lives to pay for. All in your new cell."

Playing with Fire
Tamsin Flowers

Cassandra watched as her sister got dressed, gingerly pulling the clothes up over her bruised flesh, tears streaming down her cheeks. She was pale and scrawny thin. The dark rings around her eyes made her look like a panda, and her red nail polish was chipped halfway down her bitten nails. It seemed such a short while ago that her kid sister had been a happy, healthy coed, going off to college with her friends, bubbling with laughter. Now she was a wreck, a shadow of her former self with track marks on her arms. And Cassandra held one man responsible.

The doctor handed her a prescription.

"Your sister needs to go to rehab," he said. "But if you can't afford it, you'll have to monitor her yourself. It's going to be tough on both of you."

Tough? Cassandra wondered if the doctor had any idea. She knew she needed to get Melly out of town, away from the drugs and the men who gave them to her. And away from Aston Moore, the man to whom she owed so much money and who wanted to sell her body to pay off the debt. But Cassandra wasn't stupid. She was well aware that if she didn't sort things out before they left, Moore would have them followed. He was a violent man, and Cassandra was all too familiar with his reputation, even though she'd never come across him in person.

Now, though, she had no choice.

"How much do you owe him?" Cassandra asked when they were back in the anonymous motel room, a place where Cassandra hoped Moore and his henchmen wouldn't think of looking for them.

"Stay out of it, Cass," snapped Melly, tugging her fingers through a tangle in her dirty blonde hair.

"I've got savings, Melly," said Cassandra.

"It won't be enough," said Melly. "Nothing will ever be enough for those greedy bastards. It's my mess, Cass. Please don't get involved—I don't want you hurt as well."

"You don't get a say in it, Melly. What sort of a sister would I be if I let you carry on…"

"You can't even say it, can you?"

Melly slammed the door of the bathroom behind her, and Cassandra heard the lock click into place.

✧ ✧ ✧

CASSANDRA WAS FIVE years older than her sister, Melly, and after their mother had died, she'd stood in for five years of mothering. And apparently she hadn't done a very good job. So she wasn't going to let Melly down now.

Aston Moore owned a club downtown, a strip joint or worse, where he hung out with his cronies. Cassandra had never been inside—hell, she didn't even know anyone who'd been in there. Apart from Melly. She picked her time carefully, just after lunch when the place would be quiet but not totally deserted. She picked what she was wearing even more carefully. She wanted to look tough, though she knew she'd never fool a man like Moore. But the biker boots and the ripped jeans gave her confidence, and the leather jacket was all she could use as a shield. She made up her face with harsh black kohl and dark red lipstick. She needed to be strong.

Before going to the club, she went to the savings bank and withdrew the money she had been squirreling for a rainy day. This was a bloody shit storm, and she couldn't think of a better way of spending it than helping Melly get her life back.

Cassandra's heart pounded in her chest as she walked into the dark club. Her blood thundered in her ears louder than the heavy drums and bass blasting out of the speakers at the back of the tiny stage. There was a pole, and a girl in cheap lingerie with mottled, pale skin was gyrating round it, making no attempt to keep time with the music. Most of the customers were sitting in the booths along the wall rather than within touching distance of the stage—apart from two leering older men who both had trails of spittle down their chins.

She pushed her shoulders back and strode up to the bar, where a kid who didn't appear old enough to drink was polishing glasses with a gray cloth.

"I'm looking for Mr. Moore. Is he here?"

"Depends why you want to see him," said the boy. "If you're here about dancing, you'll need to see the manager, not Mr. Moore."

"I'm not here about dancing. Like I said, I need to see Mr. Moore."

"Who's asking for me?" said a rich baritone from behind Cassandra's shoulder.

She whipped round, and she knew immediately that she was face-to-face with Aston Moore. He wasn't a big man, but the strength of his presence was undeniable. The barman melted away, and Cassandra felt herself wilt perceptibly under the glare from Moore's dark blue eyes. His features were lupine, gaunt and hollow-cheeked. His dark red lips had a cruel twist to them, and his coal-black hair was cut short and peppered with gray.

Cassandra swallowed, but she forced herself to hold his gaze.

"I'm Melly Black's sister. I understand she owes you a certain amount of money."

Aston Moore's lips quivered slightly as he looked her up and down.

"I would never have guessed you two were related," he said with a smile that didn't reach his eyes. "You look so…wholesome, compared to her."

Cassandra bit her lip, leaning forward on the balls of her feet. Anger surged through her like a torrent. It was this man's fault that her sister was a wreck, that Melly would need years of treatment and rehabilitation to get back to the way she was before.

"How much does she owe you?"

"Surely you don't expect me to know exactly how much each little druggie owes me individually?" he said. "Anyway, we have an arrangement by which she's working it off."

"At the same time as building up even more debt. I wasn't born yesterday, Mr. Moore, so don't patronize me. I'm here to clean my sister's slate, so perhaps you could go and look up, or ask whoever you need to, how much it is."

This time his smile was friendlier but still not to be trusted.

"You're a fucking firecracker compared to her, aren't you?"

"The amount?"

"It's more than you can afford."

"Try me."

As fast as a striking cobra, Moore grasped her upper arm with one hand. He pulled her close until her chest was practically touching his.

"I might just do that, Miss Black," he said. There was real menace in his voice, and Cassandra didn't have to wonder if she was getting into something that was out of her depth. "Would you mind accompanying me to my office?"

His grip on her arm gave Cassandra no real choice. He yanked her roughly away from the bar, toward a plain black door to one side of the stage. Neither the girl on the pole nor any of the clientele batted an eyelid in their direction, even as Cassandra stumbled against and upended an empty chair.

"Wait…" said Cassandra as Moore pushed against the black door with one shoulder.

He turned to look at her.

"I thought you wanted to help your sister?"

"I do but…" But she didn't trust Aston Moore.

"I don't bite," he said. "At least not until I know you better."

Reluctantly Cassandra allowed herself to be propelled through the door and into a dark corridor. Moore flicked a light switch to turn on a bare bulb hanging overhead. Along the corridor wall were photos of girls pole dancing, most completely naked and leaving absolutely nothing to the imagination. Cassandra let her gaze drop to the floor. What if one of them was Melly? Moore pushed past her to lead the way and then showed her through another door into his office. It was a small room, walls painted the same dark red as throughout the rest of the club, and a grimy window facing a brick wall did nothing to brighten the place. Moore sat behind a scarred, old-fashioned writing desk and turned on the green glass and brass banker's lamp that was the only thing to grace its surface.

"Sit," he ordered.

Cassandra did as she was told, clutching her bag in her lap and wondering where this was leading.

Aston Moore pulled a cell phone out of his pocket. "Darcy, get in here."

Within seconds the door opened and an older man stepped into the room. He had a scar on one cheek and a nose that had been broken more than once. And the cold-eyed, cynical expression of a survivor.

"Boss?"

"How much does Melly Black owe us?"

Cassandra's head jerked up at the mention of her sister's name. She looked at the man, Darcy, and wondered if he actually knew who her sister was. The glance he gave her melded sympathy and disdain in equal measure.

"Twenty-one thousand," he said without a pause for thought.

Cassandra gasped. It was far more than she'd expected. And way more than she'd ever be able to afford.

"Her payment terms?" said Moore.

"Ten hours a week on the pole until…" said Darcy.

"Whenever," said Moore. "That's all."

Darcy left and closed the door quietly behind him.

Cassandra realized she was gripping the arms of her chair with white knuckles. She made a conscious effort to relax her hands.

"Your sister's gonna be dancing here for the foreseeable future, so you better get used to the idea."

"If I can give you cash, how much will you bring the total down?" said Cassandra.

"Nothing. No discount. Just not so many hours on

the pole."

Cassandra opened her bag and drew out a brown envelope.

"Here's seven thousand dollars, Mr. Moore. I'm taking Melly away—she needs rehab. When we come back, I'll work off the other fourteen thousand if you'll promise to leave her alone."

"You ever danced?"

"How hard can it be?"

Moore's laughter rang around the small room.

"Show me," he said.

Cassandra shook her head. "I'll learn how to do it while Melly's in rehab."

Suddenly Moore was on his feet and coming round the desk toward her.

"I'm not running a fucking charity here for little junkies and their do-good sisters."

He stood above her, dark and menacing, with fiery eyes and clenched fists. She stared at him defiantly, clamping her jaw tight shut in denial of the fear welling in her gut.

"You're no dancer," he said. But he took the brown envelope from her hand and tossed it onto the desk behind him.

Cassandra let out a breath as the tension left her muscles. But his next words hit her like a punch in the guts.

"Sure you can pay off the rest of Melly's debt. On your back."

"You mean..."

He leaned forward and cut off the rest of her words by placing his mouth over hers. It might have been a kiss by name but not by intent. He pushed his tongue between her lips and plundered, rasping her chin with his stubble and not caring when his teeth clashed with hers. She felt crushed against the back of the chair, and she struggled to get a breath. His hands came to rest on her shoulders and then slid down to pin her upper arms to her sides.

"Have you ever slept with a man for money?" he whispered in her ear.

She turned her head away from him, as far round as she was able.

"Never. I'm not a whore." She had to breathe, and this close, Moore smelled good. Too good.

"Would you become one to save your precious sister?"

She remained silent, trapped in the chair as he loomed over her.

"Would you?" he prompted.

She thought of Melly and how much she'd changed. She gave a barely perceptible nod of her head. Moore stepped back, looking at her with raised eyebrows.

"Yes," she whispered. She knew she could do anything except look into Melly's sad, wounded eyes and tell her she had to come back to this place and dance the pole.

Moore returned to the far side of his desk and sat

down.

"Good," he said.

What would they be like? The men she would have to sleep with?

"This is how it's gonna work…what's your name?"

"Cassandra."

"Cassandra." He said it slowly, trying it for size. "Nice. This is how it goes down, Cassandra. I sample the goods first. Then I work out where I want to place you."

The goods? This was her body he was talking about.

"Place me?"

"I've got four clubs. Different clientele in each. They like different sorts of girls and pay a different price for their pleasure. I'm guessing you'd be right for one of my high-end clubs. But I don't do guessing—I run a business. I need to know the product I'm selling."

"So you sleep with all the girls who work for you?"

"No." The lupine grin was back in evidence. "Far from it. I usually leave that to Darcy. But you're not the usual type of girl that comes looking for this sort of work."

"I didn't come looking for it."

Moore exhaled a heavy breath.

"It's up to you, Cassandra. The money's gotta be paid back one way or another."

Cassandra bit her lip. Could she really go through with this? Prostitute herself? Sleep with men she'd never met for money? Or the alternative? Send her kid sister out stripping in front of the same men? And back into the environment that had got her hooked on drugs in the first place?

"When would we…?"

"Have the tryout? Now would be as good a time as any, don't you think, Cassandra?"

She should have been horrified, but there was something about the way he said her name that made the muscles inside her contract and made her breath catch up tight in her throat.

"N-now…?" *This wasn't how things were supposed to go.*

"The sooner you start and the better you are, the quicker you'll be able to pay it off."

Cassandra stood. She knew Moore was in total control of the situation. He held all the cards. But if she couldn't hang on to a small semblance of her own free will, she'd never be able to look herself in the eye again.

"I'll come back here this evening, Mr. Moore. That's when you can try the goods."

One dark eyebrow shot up.

"You're assuming that I'll be here this evening." His gaze slid down the length of her body with new interest. "When—and if—you start working for me, you'd better remember who's boss. D'you know Mitcham's, on State Street?"

Cassandra nodded.

"Be there at eleven. But if you're late, the deal's off and Melly will have to pay back her own debt."

⋄ ⋄ ⋄

MITCHAM'S WAS SMART, the swankiest restaurant in town. Cassandra wondered what she ought to wear. This wasn't a date. It wasn't even really a job interview—she wouldn't be paid for what she was about to do. She was going there to make herself the willing victim of extortion, to present herself to her pimp to see if she was up to the job. As she got ready, she felt sick to her stomach. But she still made an effort to look good—a body-skimming black sheath dress that flattered her figure and, underneath, her most revealing underwear. Chestnut hair tumbling in glossy curls around her shoulders, shimmering eyes and lips, a dab of perfume behind her ears. If she was hot, if Aston Moore found her attractive, perhaps he would put her to work somewhere smart, where the men would pay more. A better class of clientele? Who was she trying to kid?

At five minutes before the hour, she walked up the steps of Mitcham's, peering at the brightly lit interior through the open door. She'd never been there before—it was way beyond her budget. But she occasionally heard of people going there for a special celebration, and it featured in the local papers regularly for sponsoring a nearby children's charity. To Cassandra, it seemed a strange choice of venue for the job in hand. But maybe he owned Mitcham's too.

As soon as she stepped into the lobby, her way was barred by an officious maître d'.

"Madam, I'm sorry—the kitchen has closed for the

night," he said in a genuine French accent.

"I'm meeting Mr. Aston Moore."

His whole demeanor changed at her words.

"Please, your coat…"

The man led her through the crowded restaurant and, as they stopped to let a leaving couple pass through a gap between tables, she was able to gaze around and take in the full splendor of the place. Gilt mirrors, crystal chandeliers and the tinkle of glass and silverware—it was like a glittering golden globe, buzzing with conversation and raucous laughter. She looked around to see if she could spot Aston Moore at one of the tables, but the maître d' ushered her through a door at the far end of the dining room and then led her up a flight of stairs. On the wall an ebony sign with gold lettering pointed the way up to Private Dining. Cassandra followed nervously. While she'd been in the busy, bustling main restaurant she'd felt fine, able to believe that nothing untoward was about to happen. That she was just like any of the other diners at Mitcham's—enjoying a night out, about to meet up with a boyfriend for a late bite. But as the noise and the bright lights were extinguished by the door closing behind them, a tremor of fear traveled up her spine, and her gut roiled painfully.

Why did I come back when I could have taken Melly and run?

But she knew it would never have worked. This was the only way to extricate themselves from Moore's grasping greed. Cold dread settled in the pit of her stomach as the maître d' knocked on a door at the top of the stairs.

"Enter," said a voice from beyond.

As the man opened the door, the old man, Darcy, emerged from the room. From the way he looked her up and down, it was obvious to Cassandra that he knew exactly why she was here. Ignoring his passing stare, she took a deep breath, squared her shoulders and entered the room. It was a small dining room, all rich red brocade and gleaming mahogany, its dark velvety quiet in direct contrast to the bright, noisy room downstairs. The table still held the remnants of a dinner for several people—empty plates and glasses, a marble board on which fragments of cheese were congealing, soiled napkins strewn carelessly across plates, while unswept crumbs and spills speckled the tablecloth.

Aston Moore sat alone at the head of the table. He was dressed in black from head to toe. His jacket hung on the back of the chair, and his top few shirt buttons were undone to reveal a curl of dark chest hair. In other circumstances Cassandra would have found his looks attractive, but this evening the sight of him made her tremble.

"Ah, Cassandra, come in," he said, waving her forward. Then he looked across at the maître d', who was now standing just inside the door. "Send someone to clear away this mess, would you?"

The man nodded and disappeared, leaving Cassandra alone with the bastard who would be her pimp. *How had it come to this?* She bit her lip and stared at the floor.

"You scrub up well, but you'll get nowhere if you can't look your johns in the eye."

She raised her head and stared him in the face, hot fury coursing through her body in place of fear now.

Moore's smile was disarming, but she still glared at him.

"It's time to show me what you've got," he said, shifting in his chair as he pushed it back from the table.

"Business first," said Cassandra. "How much will be wiped off my sister's debt for every…"

"…every trick you turn?"

"Every time I have sex with one of your johns." Even just saying the words left a bad taste in her mouth.

"I can't tell you that until I've sampled the goods," he replied.

"Do I get paid for this time?"

"Listen, honey. I'm doing you a big favor here. Don't push your luck."

He was doing her a favor?

The door opened, and a waitress came in. She started clearing the table, and while she was in the room, Cassandra and Aston Moore contemplated each other in silence. A shifty, nervous silence, with tension thickening the air. The waitress seemed to pick up on it, clattering the crockery with nervous hands as she loaded her tray. By the time she left, Cassandra's heart was thundering in her chest.

Moore stood and went over to the door. There was a quiet double click, and Cassandra realized he'd locked it.

"Here?" she said. "There's no bed."

"Perhaps I could take you bent over the table," said Moore. He advanced toward her, and Cassandra stepped away. "Or I could sit back and relax in the chair while you worked on your knees. What do you think? How would you pleasure me if I was a paying client?"

Cassandra's mouth was dry. Words wouldn't form, but she could hardly think of what to say anyway. All afternoon she'd been imagining what she would need to do once she was alone with this man, a man whom she quite literally despised, but through all those hours her mind had gone blank every time she reached this moment. And now he was asking her to take the initiative.

Melly's gaunt face flashed before her eyes.

Swallowing her pride, her nerves and her distaste, she took a step toward Aston Moore, who stood his ground, watching her with an amused expression on his face.

"If you were my client, I'd ask you what your pleasure was," she said. She'd dropped her voice an octave, making it low and throaty. She put her hands on his shoulders and let them rove back and forth around his neck and down onto his chest. "What can I do to make you happy, Aston? To make you feel good?"

She dropped a hand down and pressed it against his

groin. He was semihard already, and his cock twitched at her touch. Moore looked momentarily surprised, but then he grinned.

"I'm tired, Cassandra, and a little jaded. I've had more women than you could ever imagine. I want something special, something I'll remember, that'll make me want to come back for more."

Cassandra had no idea what to do next. She was winging it. Her sexual experience heretofore came nowhere close to this. What the hell did a man like Aston Moore want? Or need? Slowly and deliberately she unbuttoned his shirt, sliding her fingers under the cool cotton and scraping her nails over his taut abs. She heard his breath catch in his throat as she eased the fabric out from the waistband of his pants. As she pushed his shirt collar back over his shoulders, she pressed her lips against his ear.

"Bitter or sweet?" she whispered.

"Bitter?" he said, sounding unsure.

"Light or dark?" she whispered.

"Dark." She could hear the smile in his voice. He was intrigued.

"Obey or be obeyed?" she whispered.

"Obey." He seemed to falter, but he left it at *obey*.

"Dangerous or safe?" she whispered.

"Dangerous," he said, grabbing a handful of her hair and yanking her head back so he could see her face. "But I think you're playing with fire, Cassandra."

"Undoubtedly," she said.

"And someone could get burnt."

"I hope so."

Then she took possession of his mouth, a rough, savage kiss with no concessions to his position as the man, the john, the paying customer, the pimp. She needed to take control and stay in control if she was going to make it through. Their lips collided as she pushed her tongue in deep, and the taste of him unexpectedly turned her on. She held the back of his neck with both hands and took her time over his mouth. His hands dropped to small of her back, and he pressed her against his body. Against the hard outline of his cock.

So she was doing something right.

She pulled back from him, stumbling slightly as they broke apart. Without his shirt, the veneer of sophistication had gone. Underneath lay a powerful landscape of sinew, bone and muscle. No to mention scar tissue. A long red welt ran diagonally across his left pec, dropping down to cut right across his nipple before curving away under his arm. On the other side, below his ribs, a starburst of raised, white skin told of a wound of a different kind. Aston Moore had won his power the hard way, the old-fashioned way. Violence was as commonplace in his world as it was rare in her own. The scars made Cassandra wonder how short his fuse was.

"Undress," she snapped at him. "All the way."

A slow smile spread across his face.

"You chose to obey, didn't you?" she said.

"I did." He let his trousers drop to the floor. His legs were strong and his hips narrow, but Cassandra's attention was most caught by the bounce of his cock as it sprang free of restraint and stood out proud from him. "Do I need a safe word?"

"You wanted it dangerous," said Cassandra.

He nodded, watching her. Waiting for her next move.

Cassandra swept the tablecloth from the table, letting candlesticks and cruet crash to the floor.

"Get up," she said, indicating the gleaming mahogany surface with a touch of her palm. The wood felt cold and hard against it. "On your back."

She didn't really expect Moore to do as she said, but he did, sitting on the edge of the table and then swinging his legs up so he was lying on his back in the center of the board. He was well over six feet tall, but the table was large enough to accommodate his full height. Cassandra quickly gathered what she needed from around the room. She would have to climb on the table and straddle him for what she had planned, so she lifted the tight shift dress over her head and let it drop to the floor. She revealed the black lace matching underwear she'd found at the back of her drawer, where she'd stashed it along with the memories of the only time she'd worn it. Wearing a matching set was a rarity for her, but putting it on had actually made her feel sexy—and Moore's appreciative grunt reinforced what she'd felt earlier.

"Don't speak," she said.

Moore remained silent as she blindfolded him with a discarded napkin.

Now she was ready to take the biggest gamble of her life. She struck a match and lit one of the candles that had rolled onto the floor the moment before. The sound of the strike was a giveaway, and she saw Moore's chest inflate as he caught his breath. But he didn't speak. Just lay there waiting with, if anything, an even harder erection. Cassandra climbed onto the table and straddled his hips. She held the candle in one hand. With the other she gently explored the scar tissue on his chest and abdomen. His cock jolted up at her touch, pressing against the soft silk gusset of her panties. She bent forward to kiss him on the mouth, and his hands went to her hips.

"Don't touch me," she whispered, "or you won't get what you need." She forced a tone of menace into her voice, and his hands dropped away.

"Good boy," she said and bit his earlobe as hard as she dared. He writhed underneath her, and his hips pushed against hers.

Cassandra straightened up and held the candle a foot above his chest. She tilted it to melt the wax faster, and within seconds it started dripping off the end, onto Moore's olive skin. As the first drop landed, he let out a yelp of surprise, his fists balling and his arms lifting defensively. But with a deep breath, he immediately placed his palms flat on the table as Cassandra moved the candle above him to make a path of waxy red orbs across the patch of dark hair at the top of his chest.

As she worked, his breathing became faster. She held the candle closer until the searing burn of the molten wax made him groan. Working slowly, she traced a pattern across his pecs, not caring when the hot wax touched the red scar tissue, not caring when he winced and bit his lip until she saw blood seeping out between his teeth. His cock told a different story. It grew long and hard. The top darkened, and his hips rolled against her as he instinctively tried to drive himself into her. But not yet. He couldn't have her until she'd finished her game.

She traced her sister's name in burning drops, but if Moore realized what she was up to, he gave no sign of it. Seeing Melly's name burned onto the bastard's chest gave Cassandra a satisfaction she'd never expected to experience this evening. But she knew she was taking a massive risk, so as soon as it was complete, she tilted the candle more steeply to make the wax run faster. Then she retraced her path with twists and curlicues and random patterns, obliterating the message she'd left on his skin, widening the area she covered and making narrow trails of wax down his stomach toward where his cock danced its eager dance.

When his every breath became a moan, Cassandra blew out the candle and tossed it to the floor. She leaned forward with her hands on his shoulders and used her teeth to raise his blindfold. He blinked, unaccustomed to the light, staring up at her before glancing at the wax patterns that ornamented his torso.

"Beautiful," he whispered.

Cassandra raised herself to kneel high above him and quickly slipped off her bra.

Moore whimpered.

"Please…"

"You want me?"

He nodded.

"Tell me how much."

"More than I've ever wanted any woman," he said, his voice hoarse with longing.

His hands came up behind her hips, and he yanked her panties down, ripping them when he couldn't get them out of the way. Cassandra was ready for him—and now she wanted him. She took his cock in one hand and held it steady so she could sink down onto him. He was large, but the force of gravity let her slide easily over his heft, the fit so tight that they gasped in unison. Slowly she pulled away and impaled herself again. And then again. And each plunge was accompanied by a grunt or a moan as Moore's hips pushed up to meet her and his hands rammed her down hard onto him.

And all the while he was staring at her face, never closing his eyes, never taking his gaze from hers. He moaned and winced and bit his lip. And finally he came with a roar so elemental that the sheer thrill of knowing she had caused it tipped Cassandra over the edge too.

She rode his cock, clenching her muscles tight as if she never wanted to let him go.

Would this be the only time?

When his hands grew slack and slipped down her thighs, she leaned forward and rested against his chest. He stroked her hair in a gesture that surprised her more than anything else about him since she'd met him. Almost tender, just for a moment. Then he rolled her off him onto the hard cold surface of the table and swung himself round so he was first sitting on the edge and then standing back on the floor.

Cassandra sat up and watched him. He walked across to the window and looked out into the darkness between a crack in the curtains.

"Get dressed and go," he said, not turning to look at her.

"How much?" said Cassandra. "How much each time?"

"I'll be in touch."

Cassandra dressed as fast as she could, stuffing the ripped panties into her bag and pulling the door open with one hand as she smoothed her dress down with the other. She couldn't get out of the place quick enough.

Has the gamble paid off?

Melly was asleep when she got back to the motel. Or, more accurately, sedated by the prescription drugs she'd been given to replace the street drugs. Cassandra doubted they were really any better. She showered and shoved her soiled clothes under the bed—she'd deal with them in the morning—but she couldn't sleep. When she closed her eyes, all she saw was the name written in wax across Moore's chest. And the scars. The marks of who he was. The wax with which she'd branded him wouldn't leave a mark beyond a couple of days, but maybe that was enough.

Maybe it wasn't.

At seven in the morning, after a snatched hour of sleep, her phone buzzed her awake with a text notification. She grabbed it and peered at the fluorescent screen. The text was from a number she didn't recognize.

Paid in full.

Want more from Tamsin Flowers? Read ALCHEMY XII – NEW YEAR'S EVE, the first episode of an exciting BDSM series.

Disposing of Donnie

Elizabeth Coldwell

"So you see, Mr. Mackenzie, life would be so much easier if Donnie wasn't around anymore."

Luanne Palmer gazed at me across the diner's table, looking up through mascara-thick eyelashes, her expression imploring. I'd seen that look from women before, and I'd never been able to resist its lure.

"Yeah, I see exactly what you mean—and please, call me Mike."

"So you think you can do it for me, Mike? Kill the lousy son of a bitch?"

Her voice had risen, thick with passion and contempt, and I shushed her, afraid of anyone overhearing even though I'd picked the booth farthest from the counter for our little rendezvous. Glancing round, I saw that no one was paying us the least mind, and I relaxed a fraction.

I'd chosen to meet her at Nardiello's for a couple of reasons. First, the diner was always quiet in the middle of the day, with less chance of any prospective client being spotted in my company. Second, they did the best damn apple pie in the state, so at least I'd get to eat well if Luanne Palmer turned out to be a no-show. God knows I'd had enough of those over the years: fantasists and time wasters who poured their hearts out over the phone to me about the man who just had to die, but lost their nerve at the last moment or couldn't come up with the necessary green to turn that fantasy into reality.

But when Luanne had come clicking into Nardiello's on those sky-high heels, body hugged by a cute polka-dot blouse and black pencil skirt and eyes disguised behind dark glasses, I knew everything about this dame was serious. The wiggle in her walk had my cock lurching to attention in my underwear, and when she'd sat down opposite me, I'd caught a whiff of a perfume that spoke of midnight and sin.

Preliminary introductions concluded, she'd assured me that no one knew she'd come here. Her husband was away on business, and she'd told the maid she was going into Charleston for lunch with an old girlfriend. Almost before the waitress had finished taking our order, Luanne had launched into a story I could have recited for her, I'd heard it so many times before. She'd been married straight out of high school to an older guy who satisfied all her material needs but not her physical ones. It was an arrangement that should have worked—he had the wife who made heads turn when she walked into a room on his arm, and she had financial security and high standing in the community. For most women, that was enough. But not Luanne.

"You know, I can't remember the last time he

touched me." She sighed. "And I can probably count the number of times we've fucked in the last couple of years on the fingers of one hand."

It seemed wrong for someone so ladylike to use a word as downright filthy as *fucked,* but I couldn't deny I didn't like the effect it had on my cock.

"Some gals wouldn't have a problem with that," I pointed out.

"Maybe so, Mr. Mac—Mike. But I have urges, you know? An itch that needs to be scratched."

And it was being scratched; I was all too certain of that. This was always the unspoken part of the story: some guy stepping in to provide the services Hubby no longer would, or could. Sometimes it was the pool boy, sometimes an old high school boyfriend. But he was always there, waiting for the day the sole impediment to their new life together had been permanently removed.

I watched the ice cream melt on top of my pie, sticky yellow rivulets trickling down the crisp pastry. "Pardon me for asking, but have you considered getting a divorce?"

Luanne shook her head. "Donnie would never agree to that. He's very old-fashioned in these matters. Marriage is for life, as far as he's concerned." She paused to suck up her root beer float through a straw, her bubble-gum-pink gloss almost demanding to be kissed right off those pouting lips. "And so I thought if I can't shorten our marriage, then the only thing I can do is shorten his life."

Put like that, it seemed almost logical. But I needed people to keep making this kind of decision. They kept me in business.

"Plus," she continued, "Donnie has a big life insurance policy, and I'm the beneficiary. So even after he's gone, he'll still be keeping me in the manner to which I've become accustomed."

"How did you find out about me?" I asked, forking up a piece of my pie. Catching sight of my reflection in the diner window, I saw sweat beading above the collar of my shirt. Even this late in September, the temperature was still in the nineties, and the slowly turning ceiling fan was doing nothing to cool me down. Unseasonable heat like this could make a man—or woman—do something they might later regret. Luanne Palmer didn't strike me as a woman who had any regrets about her decision, but I had to make sure. Once the deed was done, she wouldn't be able to change her mind.

"Oh, you come highly recommended, Mike. *Highly* recommended. All you need to know is that Marcie Willington is a good friend of mine."

I knew Marcie all too well. Nine months ago, she'd asked me to sort out her own marital problems. A few days later, her husband and I had gone out for a friendly game of golf together. Only one of us had completed the round.

"Well, that just leaves one last question. I hate to be indelicate, but do you have the cash?"

Reaching for her purse, she took out a fat brown envelope. She pushed it across the table toward me as if it was red-hot. "Just like we agreed. Half now, and the rest when the job's done."

I didn't bother to count it, just tucked it in the inside pocket of my jacket. Nothing was guaranteed to draw more attention to yourself than rifling through a pile of unmarked twenties in public.

For the first time, she turned the questions on me. "So how—how does this work, exactly? Where are you going to do it?"

"Look, Luanne, for your sake it's best if you don't know too much. If the police come asking questions—and they will—you don't want to let slip anything that might connect you to his disappearance. All I need to know is whether there's anywhere he goes on a regular basis, anywhere I might accidentally bump into him."

She sipped her drink, flipping through some social calendar in her head. "Well, he does like to go to the Elliot on Fridays, meet with clients there. It's that fancy hotel on the edge of town, you know it?"

I shook my head. "No, but I'll find it. I just need to know who I'm looking for."

Her icy demeanor cracked, and it struck me, beneath the artfully applied makeup and the expensive clothes, just how young she really was. Too young, I couldn't help thinking, to be wanting her husband dead. But business was business; I didn't judge and I didn't condemn. I knew there were parts of any story I would never be told, and to keep my conscience clean, that was the way I liked it.

"Of course." Opening the purse again, she handed me a snapshot. I knew what to expect: some fat slob, a good twenty years older than his wife, who'd let himself go to seed while expecting her to keep her figure trim and her grooming impeccable. Donnie Palmer was none of those things. His smile was that of a matinee idol, his dark hair cut in a boyish style. If anything, the average observer would consider him even more attractive than Luanne. Something about this whole scenario didn't quite add up, but my client wanted him out of the way, and what my clients want, they get.

"Can I keep this?" When she nodded, I tucked it in my wallet.

"Just one last thing..." Luanne lowered her voice, forcing me to lean closer to her. Her blouse was open one button lower than was strictly necessary, even in this heat, and I caught a glimpse of the tops of her breasts, cradled in a cream lace bra. Beneath the seductive perfume she wore, I smelled pure female, ripe and intoxicating. How Donnie Palmer could ignore this simmering little sexpot, I had no idea, but all too often you failed to see what was right under your nose.

She licked those glossy lips. "I want to thank you...Mike. You can't know how much what you're about to do means to me."

As she spoke, she slipped a hand under the table and let her palm rest on the bulge in my pants. My breath caught in my throat, but I didn't make any attempt to remove her hand. She curled her fingers, cupping me, and applied just enough pressure to take her touch from curious to exquisite. I couldn't make a sound, couldn't alert anyone to what she was doing. If she wanted to jerk me off, right here where I sat, I knew I wasn't going to do a damn thing to stop her.

"You like that, don't you?" Those slender fingers worked back and forth, taking me closer to the edge. I clutched my dessert spoon so hard I thought I might snap it in half, fighting to retain some measure of control.

"God, yes," I replied, the sound coming out as a strangled moan. I was helpless, and she knew it.

"Well, you know the terms of the contract, don't you?" She grinned, revealing small white teeth. "Half now, and the rest when the job's done."

With that, she pulled her hand away and stood. Confident she had me just where she wanted me, she turned and walked away, my last sight of her that round little ass of hers swaying in that tight-fitting skirt.

I sat for a long time after she'd gone, partly because I was mulling over when and how I was going to make the necessarily brief acquaintance of Donnie Palmer, but mostly because Luanne had induced a hard-on in me that just wouldn't quit. That cool, calculating smile of hers burned in my memory, just as the envelope of cash seemed to burn in my top pocket, and I began to wonder if I hadn't somehow got in over my head.

✧ ✧ ✧

THE ELLIOT HOTEL stood in its own grounds, a relic of a bygone age. It gave off the air of having seen better days—the potted palms in the lobby were withered and brown, and the whole place needed a lick of paint—but I wasn't there to check in. Luanne had told me her husband liked to drink here after work, and if I was lucky, he would be drinking here alone.

I spotted him almost at once, his good looks and well-cut suit a beacon of Hollywood glamour in these faded surroundings. He was sitting at the bar, nursing a glass of what looked like bourbon and staring into its depths as though it might contain the secret to all his troubles. Though why a guy as handsome and successful as Donnie Palmer had troubles, God alone knew. Maybe on a subconscious level he knew his wife wanted him dead.

Hopping onto the empty stool by his side, I attracted the attention of an elderly, white-jacketed barman who looked like he'd been serving drinks here since the day the hotel opened. He set down a white paper coaster before me. "What can I get you, sir?"

"Scotch on the rocks," I requested, slapping a couple of bills down on the counter to pay for the drink.

Once he'd served it to me, I took a long, contemplative sip, pondering my opening gambit with Palmer. Not every man likes to be interrupted when he's drinking alone, but I didn't get that vibe from him.

"Excuse me," I said, catching his eye as he looked up

from his almost empty glass, "you wouldn't happen to know if there's anywhere decent around here to get a bite to eat, would you?"

He turned that dazzling smile on me, seeming happy to be distracted from his thoughts. "That depends on what you're looking for. The restaurant here's pretty good if you like your seafood, but if you just want a burger, then I'd recommend Buddy's, about a mile back on the highway. You probably passed it if you were coming out from Charleston."

I made a show of thinking about it. "Yeah, I saw the place." Gesturing to his glass, I said, "Can I get you another?"

He considered it, then nodded. "Sure, why not? It's not like I have anything to rush home for."

"Don't tell me, trouble in paradise." I chuckled, letting him gain the impression I'd been there myself.

"You know it." The barman set another bourbon, no ice, down in front of him. He raised his glass to me in a salute. "I'm Donnie, by the way."

"Mike." I held out a hand for him to shake. As our fingers touched, a kind of electricity seemed to crackle between us. It had been a while since any man had caused that reaction in me, and part of me welcomed it, even as I was pondering the absurdity of being turned on by a guy I'd been contracted to kill. "So, what's the little lady done to leave you drowning your sorrows?"

He shrugged. "Oh, you don't want to hear about that." When I just kept staring at him, he said, "OK, but there's very little to tell. I'm just another guy who thought getting married would solve all his problems, and found all it did was cause a whole 'nother set of them. Don't get me wrong, my wife's a gorgeous, sexy little thing, but she's just not right for me. More than that, I'm fairly sure she's cheating on me."

"And that bothers you?"

"To be honest, not half as much as it should."

"Well, she's a fool," I declared. "Seems to me like any woman would be glad to have a guy like you in her life."

Donnie gave a bitter laugh. "Yeah, that's what my mom said." He glanced at his glass as if surprised how much he had downed in two long gulps; then he fixed me with his hazel eyes. The look he gave me was filled with a plea for understanding. More than that, it was filled with naked longing.

"Well, you wouldn't want to disappoint your mother, would you?"

Donnie spoke so low that I could barely hear it. "If my parents knew the truth about my marriage—hell, the truth about me—they wouldn't just be disappointed. They'd have me driven out of the county. They wanted me to settle down with a nice girl. How could I tell them what I really want is to settle down with someone like you?" He finished off the rest of his drink, clearly regretting what he'd just said.

Now I knew why Donnie Palmer was so resistant to the idea of a divorce. His marriage to Luanne provided the perfect smoke screen. No one would ever think to question his sexuality, not when he had such a hot little wife by his side. He didn't have to tell me why he came here every Friday night—or those other nights, when he told Luanne he was meeting a client. He was looking to pick up some guy like me, some passing stranger he'd never see again.

In that moment, I knew I had a choice: I could sit here plying the guy with bourbon until he was too drunk to do anything but lead me out to some dark, secluded spot where I would put a bullet in his brain, or I could have a little fun before I disposed of him. It had been a while since I'd been with another guy, but I loved sticking my cock in a tight male asshole just as much as I loved fucking pussy, and this opportunity was just too good to pass up.

I reached for my drink, brushing the back of his palm with my fingers as I did so. To anyone watching, the contact would have looked accidental, but we both knew I meant it.

"Do you want me to see if I can get us a room?" I asked.

He nodded, and I wondered how many times he'd done this before. I swallowed the last of my scotch and wandered out to the lobby. A brief negotiation with the clerk on the front desk, and I had the key to Room 12 in my hand. If he'd noticed I had no luggage, he said nothing. Maybe illicit assignations were what kept this shabby old hotel in business.

I returned to Donnie, whose face lit up as I approached. Had he seriously believed I might bail on him?

"Room 12," I murmured in his ear. "Give it five minutes, then come up and knock on the door. That way, if there's anyone here who knows your wife, they won't realize we're together."

He snorted, and I wondered if he was already a little drunker than I'd given him credit for. "Don't worry; no one here knows Luanne."

But he sat obediently on his stool, giving me time to make my way up in the creaking elevator to the third floor and let myself into Room 12. In common with the rest of the hotel, there was no air-conditioning, and I threw open the window here, hoping to let some cool air into the stuffy room. I loosened my tie, splashed cold water on my face, adjusted my burgeoning erection and waited for Donnie to arrive.

After what must have been a good ten minutes, I was starting to think he'd got cold feet. *Should have just taken him out into the garden and offed him among the rhododendrons like you planned to all along,* I chided myself. Then I heard a tentative knock. Walking over to the door, I pulled it open and practically hauled Donnie into the room.

"Thought you weren't gonna show," I said, trying to hide my impatience.

"Sorry. I bumped into someone I know from the golf club downstairs. Just couldn't shake him off. Some guys just can't take a hint, right?" He was babbling, anxious, and that anxiety was contagious. I knew only one way to shut him up. I pressed my lips to his in a long, deep kiss.

If I'd had any worries he might have been having second thoughts, they vanished in that moment. Donnie responded with passion, pushing his tongue into my mouth in an overeager but endearing kind of way. His mouth tasted of bourbon, and he was making little sighing noises into my mouth.

He didn't object as I marched him steadily backward till his back pressed against the wall. My crotch ground against his, his cock as rigid and excited as my own. We fumbled at each other's clothing, him tugging at the belt of my pants, me making short order of the buttons on his white work shirt. Donnie's chest was covered in a mat of dark curls; his belly was flat. How I ever thought I'd be dealing with some ignorant, out-of-shape schlub, I didn't know. This guy would have been totally right for Luanne, if only he hadn't been as interested in other men as she was.

"Oh God, Mike, I want you so much," Donnie moaned as he broke the kiss. He'd undone my zipper and reached into my jockeys to curl his hand around the hot bar of my cock. His touch was as sure as Luanne's had been, and I couldn't help wondering what it would be like to have both of them here, working on my length with their skillful fingers. I only hoped that, unlike his wife, he wasn't going to leave me hanging.

That thought was banished as Donnie spun me round so now I had my back to the wall. He dropped to his knees, half-naked on the threadbare carpet. He'd unfastened his own pants, and his dick stood up, curving slightly away from his body. Its length and thickness took my breath away, and I itched to have it sliding into the tight recess of my asshole, filling me like I hadn't been filled in quite some time.

Donnie had other ideas of how to pleasure me, though. Never breaking eye contact, he took the tip of my dick in his mouth and swallowed maybe a couple of inches of my hot, aching meat. Being sucked into that slick cavern almost made me shoot my load where I stood.

"Fuck, that's so good," I moaned, swept away by the feel of his tongue swirling over and around my helmet.

"You like that, huh?" he asked, letting me slip out of his mouth for a moment. He looked up at me with puppyish eagerness, seeking my approval. It was kinda pathetic: the guy should have had everything, and yet here he was, trapped in a marriage with a woman he'd married for appearances' sake and reduced to seeking pleasure with strangers in hotel rooms. It was a dangerous game; he couldn't know quite how dangerous. Yet, despite everything, I couldn't help feeling sorry for him.

"You like it?" he repeated, and I noticed he had his cock in his fist and was slowly stroking it back and forth.

"Yeah, just keep doing it like that," I told him. At once, he wrapped his lips around my tip again, taking me farther in this time. His dark head bobbed up and down my shaft as he gradually worked me into his throat. The wet suction had the juices fizzing in my balls, seeking release. The room was silent apart from the little moans he was making around my meat, and the slapping sound of his hand beating his dick. I threw my head back and let out a groan, certain I could feel Donnie smiling in response around my deeply buried cock.

Lost in bliss as I was, I couldn't afford to lose sight of why I'd brought him up here. My gun was a reassuring bulge in my jacket pocket. It would be so easy to just reach for it and press it to Donnie's temple. One squeeze of the trigger and I would blow him away, even as he was blowing me.

But I knew I couldn't do it. No man with a mouth this talented deserved to die. Sure, he was living a lie, sneaking around to find forbidden pleasure behind his wife's back, but Donnie Palmer wasn't the villain here. Indeed, as the come shot from the end of my dick and splashed over Donnie's tonsils, I knew what the real outcome of this sorry little escapade needed to be.

✧ ✧ ✧

LUANNE DIDN'T BAT an eyelid as she opened the door to me. "I take it you've come for the rest of your money." No *what happened?* Not even a shred of concern for her husband's fate. She just smiled that cold smile at me, like this was the moment she'd been waiting for her whole life.

"I found Donnie at the Elliot, just where you said he'd be," I told her as she led me into the house. As I watched her swaying ass, it was all too obvious she had nothing on under the silky red robe she wore. A couple days ago, the thought of her making good on what she'd promised me in the diner would have had me itching to shuck that robe off her shoulders, but after what had happened with her husband, the prospect no longer had the same appeal.

"Yeah, I thought you might. Always was a creature of habit, was Donnie."

The interior of the house was oppressively warm, and I wiped beads of sweat from my neck. "Say, I couldn't trouble you for a glass of water, could I?"

"Sure, come through to the kitchen."

I leaned against the kitchen table, watching Luanne as she reached into the fridge and took out a pitcher of iced water. When she turned back to me, she didn't register the gun I pointed at her until it was too late.

"I'm sorry about this, Luanne, really I am. But it's for the best all round." I took aim and fired. A small, red circle appeared on her forehead, as round and perfect as the O of her surprised mouth. The pitcher dropped from her grasp, shattering on the floor. She crumpled to the linoleum with barely a sigh, as beautiful in death as she had been in life.

I turned and walked out of the house without a backward glance. No one had seen me arrive; my fingerprints marked nothing, and no one would have the faintest clue that I'd ever been here.

All I had to do now was wait for Donnie's call. I knew it would come; his eagerness to see me again when I'd left him at the Elliot, naked, satisfied and very much alive, had been proof enough of that. More than that, he was going to need some consolation when he found his wife's body, and I was just the man to give it to him.

SURPRISE WITNESS
Audrey Lusk

"Alma, give me five minutes, undisturbed," I ordered, firmly closing the door of my office before my assistant could respond. Woman was paid enough for rudeness. Why waste sentiment?

I smiled, alone, as I never did in front of anyone—clients, colleagues, even the few I vaguely thought of as friends. Today was one of my visits. Some people meditated, some drank. I…well, recently I'd discovered this new hobby. Spike. In prison for life, Spike had this arrangement with an obsessively voyeuristic guard at the prison—at least when I made one of my visits. Shortly after our first…encounter…I took my personal interest in Spike up a notch and parlayed him into a useful informant.

I got all sorts of good prison gossip, dirt I could exchange to help my other clients, and Spike, well, he got me. And I also got…stress relief…in the form of rough, nasty, intense sex. I supposed I might feel ashamed about how thrilling I found it to be abused by someone I should've held nothing but contempt for, but frankly that would be as much of a waste as sympathy for my secretary.

Everyone I worked with, everyone I casually encountered took one look and saw an ice queen, a bitch with brass balls, someone who could very possibly make hell freeze over with a stray glare.

I worked hard for that.

I was stripping out of my good hose and changing into an old silk blouse, suitable for roughhousing, when a knock came at the door. I ignored it. Considered firing my assistant for her failure to run interference.

"Diane?" A junior-partner voice if I ever heard one. Glen Openshaw. I couldn't ignore him, but I could make him wait. "Diane?" His voice was as bland and forgettable as his face, his personality. A Ken doll made flesh. I imagined his smooth dickless crotch—then imagined setting it on fire.

I tucked in the blouse, stepped back into my shoes without hose and stormed to the door, throwing it open. Ignoring Glen entirely, in his perfect suit and tie, his pastel shirt, I yelled, "Alma, didn't I ask for five goddamn minutes?"

"Sorry, Ms. Burke, I—"

"It's my fault." Glen made one of those conciliatory faces that gave me the urge to slap him. "I had to catch you before you left. You're going out to Millhouse today?"

The prison, yes, I thought, excitement rising within me at the mere thought of Spike and his dark marble-like eyes. None of that reached my face, though, and all

I said was, "Why?"

Glen smiled again, completely oblivious to my deep loathing. "Well, I was hoping to come along."

"No." I shut the door on him.

Glen wasn't bad looking, tall and lean from hours of obligatory Pilates or whatever. Perfect hair, perfect teeth. Bred for corporate law. I bet his daddy was a lawyer, and he never had to work a day in his life to get through college. Legacied into the right frat.

He wouldn't be so damned wishy-washy if he'd ever had to compete for anything, ever had to prove himself. Whereas, being a particularly well-endowed blonde, I had to constantly hammer home the fact that I was more than a sex kitten, a blow-up doll, a ditz joke.

Alone, I began to shake—but only on the inside. I couldn't just drop round to see Spike every week. How dare this ass try and horn in on my very precious time? No way was he going to stop me from getting what I wanted, what I craved.

Was this what it felt like to be an addict?

Probably.

Fuck it.

I quickly rolled on the new pair of cheap nylons and shrugged back into my suit jacket. It was about time to get going. Spike would be expecting me.

Glen was waiting at my car.

"Look, Diane, Meyers wants me to go with." Even though his tone was still tentative and apologetic, the bastard didn't pull any punches, citing the senior of all senior partners.

I seethed. I could feel a seethe burn over me, replacing all the tasty lust I'd been hoarding for this trip, like a good buzz gone sour.

But Meyers requires. And no one says no.

"Why?" My tone should have frozen him on the spot, but Glen hardly seemed to notice.

"Nothing about your performance, let me reassure you! Your work with Spike has been duly noted at very high levels." I would give a shit about that later, I was sure, but right now I could not have cared less.

Glen continued. "Just that I have a few questions for him that might help out another client, and I was hoping that if I went along with you, you could grease the wheels a bit. You know." He ended with a hearty self-effacing shrug.

Well, with you along, no one's getting greased. My thoughts were in capital letters with exclamation points around them. I imagined covering Glen in bacon fat and feeding him to hungry lions.

While I knew I couldn't say no, I let everything hang—just long enough to make Glen fidget. I had to get *some* satisfaction out of the day.

"Fine. Get in the car." I popped the autolocks and slid behind the wheel.

As soon as the doors were shut and seat belts on, Glen turned confidential. "Are you mad at me? This isn't because of what happened at the holiday party last year, is it?"

I would have laughed, but I was as good at suppressing *that* as I was my anger. The holiday party? I'd almost forgotten Glen's drunken pass—the sloppy beer-scented kiss, the attempt to paw me in the copy room. If he'd shown a bit of backbone, pushed harder, then maybe… What? Probably just a harassment suit. Glen was a jellyfish; Spike was a shark.

I imagined a shark eating a jellyfish with Glen's face, and almost smiled.

Besides, that was before I'd found out what I wanted, what got my starter out of neutral. What I was now craving with every fiber of my being.

Glen was waiting for an answer. Again I made him fidget.

Finally I spoke without turning my eyes from the road. "Let's just get this over with."

For most of college, I truly had been the ice queen I appeared. I tried sex a couple of times, in a couple of combinations, with mixed results, but mostly no glimmer of what the big deal was. And masturbation had seemed like a waste of good studying time. I blew guys who wouldn't take no for an answer, and made all the right noises when they groped me, and never went back for more.

Turned out, they just didn't have the right approach.

Sitting in the attorney consultation room, Glen tried again with the small talk. "So this Spike must respect you, really be impressed by your professionalism. He's supposed to be such a hard case."

Can't you just shut up? my mind was screaming. I found an image to cheer and comfort me, a vision of Glen in a ball gag, something I'd only ever seen in movies, and was almost able to smile if I had wanted to. Instead I busied myself with removing my jacket, draping it carefully over the back of the chair.

The door opened, and Spike, in his typical disrespectful slouch, was ushered in by his pet guard Lewis. I tightened at the sight of him—orange jumpsuit loose around his hips, white wifebeater displaying his extensive collection of cheap prison ink, blue on pale indoors-only skin. Just the sight of his shaved head and impressive ropy muscles frustrated me with superfluous wetness. Gassing up the car to leave it in the fucking garage.

Walking in on *us* instead of *me,* Spike's reaction was almost invisible—a slight hitch in his step, a tightening of the muscles at his jaw, a slitting of his normally hooded dark eyes.

Lewis, the guard, was less subtle—with a gape of disappointment that he tried to cover up with the most pathetic fake yawn ever. Didn't matter. Glen was clueless and I was fuming.

As Lewis shut the door, Spike flung himself into the chair across the table from mine and stared at me. I matched his furious glare, trying to convey that this was neither my choice nor my fault. I won't say that there was an unspoken conversation or an instant understanding or anything so unanimous, but his lizard-like expressionless eyes slid to Glen for a hair of a second, and I dipped my eyes in a non-nod.

The silence stretched on until Glen, oblivious, half stood and extended a hand across the table. "It's nice to finally meet you, Mr., uh, Spike. I'm Glen Openshaw."

Spike didn't spare a single glance for Glen. "What the fuck is this?" His voice was even—low and dangerous like the buzz of a distant chain saw hitting no resistance.

I let my annoyance seep through, shifting the blame. "Glen has a client who needs a name. *He* thought he'd have a better chance of convincing you if he came along when I was here."

Spike held my gaze for another eternity, which probably lasted thirty seconds. The very cold and calculating nature of his stare didn't unnerve or frighten me so much as get me hot. Perhaps that was what made us so well suited for each other—we were both wound so tight, hiding every scrap of weakness, of emotion, we'd snap if we didn't have the chance to cut loose from time to time.

Finally, I saw his lips twitch in a flicker of a smile, and my guts rolled over in thwarted anticipation.

Spike finally turned his reptilian gaze to Glen. "You think you have something better to offer? Do you even know how she 'squeezes' so much dirt out of me?"

Glen opened his mouth to speak, but nothing came out. He just gaped when Spike stood, revealing his long, hard, veiny cock sticking out above the bunched baggy orange jumpsuit.

Before Glen could breathe, much less react, Spike's long wiry arm snapped across the table, catching me by the hair. I let him drag me out of my seat and forward to lie across the table, my mouth in perfect position for his throbbing cock. My gasp was rudely interrupted by the hard thrusting intrusion, choking me in the best possible way. I shuddered with the need it aroused, making my entire body hum.

I didn't try to imagine what Glen might be thinking—particularly after his own clumsy Yule-fueled pass—but I heard him begin to sputter. I was just happy that I was still going to get my playdate, topped with the thrill of making straightlaced, vanilla, Ken doll Glen participate, even if only by watching.

Spike's voice cut through the bluster, cold as hell, even as he began humping his cock in and out of my tight sucking lips. "So, Glen, what you got to top this?" For one dark moment, I flashed on the thought that he might prefer to abuse Glen—you know what they say about prison—and found myself almost jealous. Spike's grip tightened in my hair, though, and I felt his cock twitch in my mouth. I figured that was about all the encouragement I'd ever get from him, and took it as a good sign.

I couldn't see Glen from my extreme angle but filled in details in my imagination—picturing him bug-eyed and sweating, hopelessly turned on by watching me getting face fucked this way. I had to add a dick to my internal picture of him, and it wasn't very big, but it was screaming… I hummed happily on Spike's cock and got an extra-tight squeeze on my hair in return.

Glen finally found his voice again. "Stop. That. I'll get the—"

"Yeah, right. Sit your fucking ass down or Lewis can't see, and he likes to watch." I heard Glen's chair squeak and assumed the dumb-ass obeyed, but all I could really focus on was the iron-hard rod plunging in and out of my mouth…that and keeping my lips nice and tight around it.

Spike dragged me a little farther forward, across the table, so my thighs were pressed hard against the back edge and I had to spread them to take the strain. I felt the tension vibrating his hands in my hair, and was amazed that none of it could be heard in his voice. Instead, he almost sounded disinterested. "She likes it, the horny slut. Don't believe me, Glen? Get in there and feel her cunt—she's got to be creaming by now."

I tensed, waiting for Glen's hand, wanting to feel him capitulate. To become complicit in the game. Nothing. Chickenshit. I wasn't surprised but found I was almost disappointed.

Spike was too, it seemed. "Did that sound like a request, Glen? You want my help; you better make it worth my fucking while."

An instant later, I felt Glen's fingers on the back of my knee, and it sent such a thrill through me, I almost choked on the meat in my mouth but managed to stop myself from biting down. Glen's fingers began to trace a tentative trail up the back of my leg, under my skirt, his nails making a slight skreeing noise, skimming across the cheap pantyhose.

Glen hesitated for only a second at the cotton panel covering my now soaked pussy, then pressed inward slightly, feeling the damp. I knew he felt it—I heard him gasp.

Spike had slowed his pumping slightly but was going for depth, leaving me barely able to get enough air between thrusts. "Rip your way in and get a couple of fingers into this bitch's cunt."

It took every ounce of my limited self-control to not move, to not thrust backward with my hips, to not show any interest in Glen's fingers—futilely rooting around, looking for a way through the hose.

"Pussy." Spike dismissed him, pulling me abruptly off his cock so he could look into my eyes. "Maybe this fucker just gets to watch." He didn't say it like he was asking me, just taunting Glen. "Or he can shut his eyes and listen." He chuckled almost soundlessly. "Maybe stand in the corner."

With this, I heard and felt nylon tear, and fingers invaded my steaming wet cunt. Even as I gasped, my mouth was once again filled with cock, and I was being invaded from both ends.

Glen was still fumbling, sloppily plunging two fingers in and out of my vagina, when Spike abruptly hit him with, "You like a good ass fuck?" Glen was stunned, and his hand froze, thumb pressed against the back of my thigh, sticky fingers tracing cold lines against my skin.

"No. Not *m-me*," Glen managed to stammer, fear oozing from every word. I loved it, and much as I wanted Spike's attention for myself, I still took great pleasure in a cruel image of Glen being bent over the table and taken by force, crying and orgasming all at once.

"Too bad." Spike pulled me hard against his crotch, mashing my lips into the hair at the base of his cock, choking me deliciously, then gave a long grunt and spewed a heavy load of jism deep in my throat. "If you…said yes…I woulda let you fuck her in…the ass. Guess you lose." Then he groaned again and left the last few drops on my tongue as he pulled his cock out of my mouth, leaving me desperately swallowing and gasping for air.

Glen's voice was all relief, with a new sound—an undertone of deep hunger. "Oh, like *that*—"

"Fuck you." Spike took a deep breath. "You *lose*. Sit down."

Glen tensed his hand on my ass, then shoved his fingers deep inside my pussy, defying Spike. I gasped, and my back arched up, lifting my head and shoulders off the table so my nipples, in their silk and lace casings, just brushed against the surface.

Even through half-slitted lids, I could see Spike's

eyes narrow in consideration. "Fine. You have until I get hard again to get into this bitch's ass. Ticktock ticktock." Spike's gaze moved to me. "Start sucking, cunt," as he presented his momentarily exhausted penis to my lips. I got my hands up in front of me this time and started to pump his cock, working my jaw to recover from the reaming he'd given me.

Glen flipped my skirt up over my ass, baring my split-open hose and soaking crotch. I heard more ripping as he widened the tear, then spread my thighs as far as they would go, palming my ass cheeks apart and sending a shiver up me as my tiny rosebud was exposed to the coolness of the air.

Spike pinched my ear, pulling my attention back to the cock knocking at my lips—it was already half-hard again. He was obviously enjoying watching Glen's desperate movements. I opened my mouth obediently, but he held himself back, just out of range—close enough that I could just get my lips and tongue around the knob, and I nibbled and licked as best I could, stroking the shaft with my hand.

Glen ran a finger up my wet crease to moisten it, and just as he finally pressed that bony intrusion hard into my tight little asshole, Spike shoved his cock to the root into my mouth again. The finger hurt, and when Glen pulled out and worked two of them in, the ache was terrible—and still thrilling.

Even though Glen had probably always wanted to fuck me, never in his wildest, nastiest dreams could he have thought he would be allowed—let alone forced—to sodomize me, all the while being watched by a convict who was ravaging my mouth. Forced. Yes. Poor little Glen was being forced to help rape me. That was almost as thrilling as the idea that they'd both be pumping into me at once—end to end.

Spike muttered, "Yeah, that's a fucking hot mouth, babe," then louder, "Ticktock ticktock, better hurry, Glen."

Glen groaned and began to furiously work at widening my asshole, constantly stroking through my cunt to moisten the smaller hole. Finally, I heard his zipper and felt his cock spring out, hot enough to almost burn the spot on my leg where it brushed me, making me gasp again on Spike's hard spike, and earning me an extra-deep thrust to gag me.

Then Glen shoved his cock into my pussy, hard. One thrust, then a second one, his groans so loud they drowned out the sound of my own gasping breaths. I had to amend the picture in my imagination—his dick wasn't tiny and spongy, but good and long—not too thick, but it felt like he had a huge knob on there, which would be difficult to slot into my tiny hole.

Before Spike could reprimand him, Glen shifted his now well-lubed shaft, moving it up and into position. He pressed hard but couldn't seem to make any headway. I was distracted from his clumsy efforts, though, as Spike pulled his cock out of my mouth and ran it over my lips, then rolled my head to the side and moved closer until his balls rested on my lips, demanding attention. I licked and sucked, running my fingers over his scrotum and teasingly up the length of his shaft, which earned me another twitch of that almost ready organ.

Glen shoved both thumbs into my asshole, making me squeal as he spread me as wide as he could, pressing his huge knob into the tiny gap formed by his straining digits. I had a distinct feeling he'd never done this before. And here we were, ruining him for anyone else.

I felt him pause with just the tip caught tight by my sphincter; then he pulled his thumbs out quickly. He would have lost what ground he had if Spike hadn't shoved me back hard onto Glen's fleshy prong—much to Glen's astonishment and my masochistic delight.

It hurt, but I was expecting it. Reveled in it. Took sadistic glee in Glen's willing unwillingess, and appreciated Spike's warped imagination all the more. I groaned long and deep, whether in agony or ecstasy I don't know, and reflexively tried to buck Glen loose, rearing up off the table as best I could as the huge head of his cock speared its way through my tight, protesting ring of flesh.

Spike effortlessly held me there, suspended above the table, supported by Glen's cock and one tattooed, implacable hand. With his other hand, he caught the neckline of my white silk blouse and yanked, hard, tearing the delicate fabric with a shrill zipping noise and a rattle of escaping buttons, exposing my breasts, barely controlled by a simple white lace bra.

Held in this strange half-lifted position, I felt Glen's cock slide deeper—or rather, I felt myself slide inexorably down his shaft. Once the head had passed the tight entrance, the pain lessened some. As if in reflex, Glen's hands caught convulsively at my hips, pulling me the rest of the way onto his hot member, until I could feel his expensive shirt against the soft skin of my derriere.

Spike maneuvered around the end of the table, clutching me by one shoulder and a breast, pressing me back and down. I felt like a doll, a toy, something to be used, and I reveled in the surrender of control.

We were still moving, like some weird three-person dance, until I felt jolted against Glen as we were backed into a corner. The impact drove him even farther into me, flattening my perfect buttocks against his pelvis.

I took a breath and felt Spike pull my bra down and spill both breasts out over the top. His hands clamped onto them, mauling my lovely mounds and tweaking my nipples, forcing me to wriggle and moan, each move making me more and more conscious of the cock in my rear.

Finally, Spike kicked my feet apart, then melded himself to my body, his burning cock sliding up into my well-wetted cunt in one hard thrust.

I gasped and flinched as one tattooed hand shot toward my face, but he reached past me to grab Glen's ear and pull his head forward against my shoulder. Spike hissed, "You better not fucking come until I'm done."

Glen groaned, but I felt his chin move against my bare skin as he nodded. Then Spike was moving, fucking up into me, pressing me hard against Glen, as if he was fucking us both at once. Each thrust of his nasty, hard cock hit deep inside me, rubbing against Glen's stationary member, separated as they were by the thinnest of barriers.

I took every chance to torment my erstwhile coworker, tightening and rolling my ass back and forth to meet Spike's thrusts, jerking on Glen's cock in my ass each time. Vindictive? Yes. I wanted him to fail and fail spectacularly. I made painful sexy noises, trying to push him prematurely over the edge. He was too timid to even grab my breasts, the lump.

Glenn was breathing hard in my ear, trying to hold on, but I could feel his cock twitching, could feel his muscles clenching, ready to shoot. Too bad—Spike showed no sign of letting up anytime soon. I clamped my hands on Spike's shoulders, digging my nails in, and whipped my head around, catching a glimpse of Lewis the guard, plastered to the glass of the door. I smiled at him and ran my tongue around my lips and was rewarded with a look that said he just came in his pants.

Now for Glen. I clenched my ass tight and screamed, "Oh God, Glen! You're hurting me!" And he climaxed. And he would never be able to forget *that*, I though smugly.

Glen let loose with a long gasping scream and shot a torrent of come into my ass, the hot blast starting me on a chain of orgasms, shaking and twisting and grinding my cunt on Spike's unstoppable cock. Spike pulled out of me with a juicy sticky noise, leaving me to fall forward with the lack of pressure. I felt Glen start to slump behind me, exhausted, and threw myself back against him, hard, keeping him tight against the wall so, flaccid or not, he wouldn't be able to get loose before I was good and ready.

Spike grabbed my chin and tilted my face downward to stare at the tiny slit in his glans, a couple feet below my eyes. He stroked himself, making me watch; then his body tensed, his hand sliding down to my throat and tightening as hot jets of white gooey come shot out of that slit and felt like boiling oil as it sprayed all over my belly. He snarled like an animal as he came, shooting so hard that a drop even made it up to my cheek. He kept pumping and shooting, though none of the aftershocks were anywhere near as powerful as that first one, until I was well coated.

Then he yanked off the last shreds of my blouse and wiped his cock, casually tucking himself back into his industrial oranges.

I finally released Glen, feeling him slide limply out of my ass as I stumbled toward the table, my legs buckling from the exertion and the fierce pounding of the blood in my veins. Spike shoved me, though not roughly, into a seat, and took his own place on the far side, shifting his chair with a harsh scraping noise. We both ignored Glen as he tidied himself as much as he could, then stumbled back to the table.

Glen swallowed and looked at me, though I only saw him in my peripheral vision. I sat there, the ice queen again, despite my state of dishabille—my blouse shredded and gone, my bra only a sling that my breasts were spilling out of, and my skin coated in semen. My skirt was still hiked up, and I sat bare-assed against the chair since I could still feel Glen's juices leaking out of my hole, and I wanted to avoid dry cleaning if I could.

I swiftly put my hair to rights and wiped down my torso with my ruined blouse. As if it were nothing, I slid each breast back into its cup.

Realizing he wasn't going to get any reaction from me, Glen cleared his throat and addressed Spike in a slightly high voice, a this-never-happened tone, "So, um, my client—"

Spike interrupted him, sliding his white tee off over his head as he spoke. "Fuck him. You need to work on your timing." Spike shot to his feet and threw the shirt onto the table in front of me, then strode to the door.

Glen sputtered, "But—but you—"

"Come back in a week. And you better fucking do what I say next time." With that, Spike slammed out of the room.

I slipped the wifebeater tee casually over my head, breathing in the sharp tang of Spike's sweat. My trophy. Something dark caught my eye—black ink at the bottom edge of the white cotton. Four letters.

MINE

And written upside down, so I could read it when I put it on. I suppressed a smile and quickly tucked it into my skirt, feeling Spike's mark against my skin.

Pulling on my jacket, I stood, craning my neck to see how much semen had spotted my skirt. Not too bad, I decided, then caught Glen's anxious look. "What? You came too soon. You need to work on your timing." I grabbed my case and swept out.

As we drove off in silence, I was turning over possibilities in my head. Making a list of coworkers—who else might I enjoy being forced to fuck?

LAST DAY
TRENT EVANS

ALYSON HART'S NIGHTMARE began with a simple envelope.

She arrived, late as usual, mumbling another excuse to the scowling office manager. The yellow manila waited for her on her desk. Opening the envelope, the damning contents spilling onto her cluttered desk, the certain write-up for her tardiness no longer mattered anymore.

Oh no. God, no.

The photographs trembled like leaves in the breeze as she clutched each one in shaking fingers. The note inside was scrawled in the stark block print of the CEO, Will Ellsworth. As she read it, dread sank in her belly like a cold lead weight.

"These are copies, Ms. Hart. There are more, but this is more than enough for the authorities. Be in my office at 8:30 this morning. You won't be late."

Her quaking hands stuffed everything back into the envelope, her heart pounding. She'd been so careful—

only shaving off a little here, a little there. Not much more than rounding errors in the company's books. Who would miss it? She knew she'd taken less cash than the company blew on a single off-site business meeting. Much less.

But somehow he knew. And now her life was over.

"Ms. Hart. I need to speak with you in the conference room." Connie's frown and her quiet, exasperated sigh told Alyson everything she needed to know.

"I—I can't, Connie." Alyson looked at the clock on her computer: 8:25. "Will, I mean, *Mr. Ellsworth.* He wants to see me."

"Now?" Connie lifted a sculpted brow. "Does he even know who you are?"

"I don't know." Connie's eyes slid over to the manila envelope, and Alyson snatched it up, stuffing it in her purse. "I have to go, though. He was very…specific."

The walk to Will Ellsworth's office felt like a walk to the gallows, the long sunlit corridor seeming to stretch before her forever, every step one closer to her doom.

"Uh, I'm here to see Mr. Ellsworth." Alyson stopped at the admin's desk, clasping her purse in both hands in a death grip, hoping to hide the tremor of her hands.

"You have an appointment?" Karen, his admin, lowered her glasses, the dark frames somehow charming on her delicate features.

"I'm not really sure. I was told to be here at eight thirty. Is he expecting me?"

Karen's phone buzzed, her delicate fingers picking it up. The voice on the other end was barely audible, but the rumble was definitely male.

"Yes, sir," Karen said. "She's here now."

Karen hung up, glancing up at Alyson. "He's ready for you."

The door, the blackness of the wood seeming to absorb the sunlight, swung open, and Alyson slipped in. With a sepulchral *thud*, the door closed behind her.

His corner office seemed all windows, and up here on the thirtieth floor the sunshine filled the space with dazzling light and warmth. Not what she'd expected of Will Ellsworth—the man whom many of the other accountants referred to as simply *The Unholy*.

Of course now, the only sunshine she could look forward to was that which filtered through the high narrow window of a jail cell.

Will was on the phone, his rangy, tall form sprawled in a chair behind the dark, expansive plane of his desk. His long fingers flipped and twirled an ornate pen. Deep blue eyes snapped up to her, and his mouth tightened.

"Look, Rick, I need those reports. Without that data we've got no chance at figuring out if we can get the account." Will's finger pointed at her, then jabbed down at the small gray chair before his desk.

Swallowing a frightened whimper, she took the seat, the fabric rough against her thin skirt. Her hands shook more than ever, and she clasped them in her lap, afraid to look at him as his conversation continued.

"I have to go, Rick. I don't care how you do it, but I want them by tomorrow. I pay you well for this, and I want *something* for my money. That's all."

Dropping the handset into its cradle, Will's intent gaze locked upon her. With his jet-black hair and the square jaw darkened by five o'clock shadow, he'd have seemed handsome in any other situation.

Here he seemed nothing so much as judge, jury and executioner.

"Do I not pay you well for the work you do, Ms. Hart?"

"I'm sorry?"

"Are you hard of hearing along with being a criminal?" He pulled open a drawer and placed a white business card on the varnished cherry wood, the gold filigree of his fountain pen glinting in the light. "I *said,* do I not pay you well?"

"Yes, of course."

"Then why embezzle from the company? From *me?*"

"Sir, my son and I..." She swallowed hard, knowing it was hopeless. "Since the divorce, we're barely making it, and—"

"Why didn't you ask for a raise?"

What? "I don't—What do you mean?"

"If you were hurting for money, why didn't you ask for more?"

"It's not that simple."

"It never is, is it?" His grin was devoid of warmth,

more a grimace than an expression of humor. "So you steal from me instead. Much easier, isn't that right?"

"No—"

"You saw the evidence, Ms. Hart. It's all there—and more." He stood, the movement of his body as fluid and deliberate as a leopard. He crossed his arms, the dark fitted button-down shirt outlining his muscled chest. "I need only make a single phone call, and you'll go away for five years. Maybe ten?"

"Please, Mr. Ellsworth. Please don't." Her heart felt like a wild animal frantic to beat its way out of her chest. "I'll pay it back. I'll do...*anything.*"

The glacial blue of his eyes glinted. "About that, Ms. Hart. What *are* you prepared to do to...resolve this?"

"I'll work overtime, weekends. I'll pay it all back, with interest." Her mind whirled, panicked. "Anything you need, I'll do it. Please, sir. Just give me a chance."

He walked around the end of his desk and leaned against its edge, crossing his ankles, glancing down with a shake of his head.

Please God. Please get me out of this!

Will looked upon her then, and the iciness of his gaze made tears prick at the corners of her eyes. She was doomed. What about Noah? Who would take care of him? A five-year-old with a jailbird mother, alone, the one constant in his young life locked behind bars.

"You don't deserve a second chance, Ms. Hart. And you're not getting one from me."

"Oh please," she said, her voice breaking, the tears

welling now. Her legs shook, strength draining from her. "I can't go to jail. I'll—He needs me. My Noah—"

Will's jaw clenched so hard she was sure it would break. "Quiet, Ms. Hart. I don't want to hear it."

The first tear tracked down her cheek, and she wiped it away with the back of a trembling hand.

Will stood once more, moving close, looming over her. His shirt, his slacks, all of it—fine, pressed. Perfect. The white blouse she wore had a yellow stain that refused to come out in the wash, so she'd covered it up with her black suit jacket. At least the jacket hadn't been too wrinkled. She felt like a slob next to this man.

"There may be one way you can avoid prison, Ms. Hart." His finger poked the lapel of her jacket, his gaze darkening. "I should have your ass hauled out of here in cuffs, but against my better judgment, I'm thinking of…an alternative."

"Oh thank you, Mr. Ellsworth!"

"I liked 'sir' better."

"Sorry. Sir."

She clung to that tiny bit of hope like a drowning woman, every second an eternity. Maybe she did have a chance after all?

Will drew in a breath, watching her silently a moment. "We'll see just how much you want to avoid prison, Ms. Hart."

"I'll do anything, sir," she whispered, looking down with a shaky breath. "Just tell me what to do, and I'll do it."

"You'll be *obligated* to me. In all things, Ms. Hart. Do you understand what that means?"

"I—think so, sir." She didn't really, but the thought of being penned in like a trapped rat in some godforsaken cell was much, much worse than the unknown of Will Ellsworth's offer.

"Take off your jacket."

Her eyes shot up. "Take off...?"

"Do it, or I call the cops."

"Sir, I—"

This cannot be happening. This is a dream, some kind of surreal nightmare.

"You have five seconds. Take off that fucking jacket, or we're done here."

Numb, her fingers worked at the buttons, the jacket falling to the floor. The quick beat of her heart thumped loud in her ears.

His hands took hold of her blouse, and automatically she grasped his forearms, pushing at him. "What are you doing?"

"Hands at your sides, Ms. Hart." His perfect smile flashed, the strong, white canines gleaming. "You're doing whatever the fuck you're told to do from here on out. It's that or prison. Your choice."

With a frustrated little sound, she dropped her hands, feeling the pulse pounding at her throat.

Buttons flew in all directions as he ripped the blouse open. He yanked down on each side, exposing her further, and she cried out.

His glittering gaze dropped to the white lace of her bra, her breasts heaving as she sucked in a great breath. She'd gained a couple more pounds since the divorce, the bra now not quite up to the task of containing her breasts.

"You can't—"

"Oh yes, I can, Ms. Hart."

Yanking the torn blouse from the clutch of her skirt, he ripped it down each arm in turn, pulling it from her and tossing it on his desk. He pointed down.

"Pull the skirt up and hold it at your waist."

"Wh—Right here?"

"Right here. And I'd better hear some respect in your tone, Ms. Hart. I might think better of this and call the whole thing off."

"Yes, sir," she murmured, dropping her gaze.

"I'm waiting."

She pulled her skirt up, clutching it in her fists at her hips, her cheeks heating.

"At least those panties match the bra."

"Why are you doing this?" She cleared her throat, her voice breaking. "Sir."

"Because I want to see if you'll do as you're told."

Will walked back to his chair and sat down once more, his legs extended, feet crossed. His ease galled her almost as much as her exposure.

"Drop that skirt, pick up your jacket and leave."

"What about...my blouse?"

"What about it, Ms. Hart? You've got your jacket."

Another tear rolled down her cheek as she smoothed her skirt down her thighs, stooping to snatch up her jacket. She buttoned it up quickly, then looked up at her tormentor.

"It's—it's showing too much. I can't leave here like this, sir."

The jacket was low cut, intended to be worn with a blouse or sweater. Her jiggling cleavage was entirely exposed, the bra itself barely hidden by the open neckline.

You look like a whore, Alyson.

"Not my problem." He spun in his chair, his back to her as he picked up his phone. "Get out."

"I'll pack my things, sir," she murmured, eying the ruin of her blouse lying on his desk. How was she going to walk back out there like this? At least she could pack up fast and run out.

"You aren't packing a thing. Get back to work—but not on your usual accounts." He looked back at her, his eyes blazing. "I'll have Karen send over your new assignments."

"Sir? You're not…firing me?"

"I'm not letting you out of my sight, Ms. Hart. How would I keep an eye on you if I canned you? Stop stalling and go."

"Yes, sir."

Time seemed to have slowed, the strange morning getting stranger by the second. She hurried for the exit.

"Ms. Hart?"

She looked back, her hand on the silver door handle.

The gold pen flashed in the light as he wrote something on the back of the business card, then slid it across the desk toward her.

"Take it."

The card shook as she read it. It was an address, somewhere over in the Ravenna area. Affluent, exclusive.

"What's this, sir?"

"The first day of your obligation. Tomorrow afternoon. One o'clock."

✧ ✧ ✧

STANDING ON HIS front steps, two huge evergreen trees soaring above her, she felt as if the entire city watched her, knew what she was up to. Which was ironic because *she* didn't even know what she was up to.

A car pulled to the curb behind her, the engine shutting off. Heavy steps sounded on the wooden stairs behind her; then she caught the faint, familiar sandalwood scent of Will's cologne. She dared not look at him.

His hand extended around her to the door, unlocking it and pushing it open.

"Inside. Don't touch anything."

Nodding, she stepped into the house, the interior all dark woodwork, immaculate.

The door closed behind her, the dead bolt thrown. Final.

"Down the hall. My office. First door on the right."

She felt him following close behind, her heart jackhammering faster with each step into the house.

Turn around and leave, Alyson. Go to the goddamned police. This is blackmail. This is illegal.

But so was embezzling. She'd see this through—it was her only choice, and they both knew it.

The office was small, intimate, the stout oak desk filling most of the space, three of the walls dominated by floor-to-ceiling shelves packed with books.

"Drop your jeans, and bend over the desk," he said, depositing his keys on the desktop and pulling open a long drawer. The pale length of cane he drew out made her heart leap into her throat.

"You're not going to…?"

"Oh yes, I am—unless you're backing out." His hand rested on the phone next to the computer monitor on the desk.

"No. No, I'm sorry."

"Good. Now stop stalling and do it."

Oh dear God.

Fumbling with the buttons of her jeans, she pushed them down, stooping to try to work them off over her shoes.

"No," he said. "Leave them there. I want those panties down too, then over the desk. Quickly."

Alyson chanced a glance at him. He wore one of the slim charcoal suits he favored for work, which was strange considering it was Saturday. The coat showed off the breadth of his shoulders, the fit emphasizing the way his body tapered to a slim waist.

She gulped, noting the prominent bulge at the front of his slacks. Was this retribution turning him on?

"Ms. Hart." His voice growled. "I won't ask again. Panties down and over that fucking desk."

With a whimper, she hooked her thumbs inside her panties and whisked them down, feeling as if her face might catch fire with the fierceness of her blush.

You're doing this for your son. Don't think about it. Just get it over with.

She lay over the cold desktop, burying her face in her arms. The rattan pressed to her buttocks, and she yelped.

"This is step one in satisfying your obligation to me, Ms. Hart. Do you agree to continue?"

"Yes," she whispered.

Is this really happening?

The cane snapped down, and she froze with the searing sting, then groaned as the ache sank into her flesh.

The second stroke landed, and she blew out a frantic breath, the hurt clawing into her bottom.

"How many, sir?"

"As many as I want to give you, Ms. Hart." His voice thickened. "But we'll start with ten today, since your lily-white bottom is so tender. It's about to be a lot less white and lot more tender."

The third strike made her cry out, fire lancing low across the base of her buttocks. Her knees failed her, her hips dropping as she tried to cope with the pain.

"Get that ass back up, Ms. Hart. We're not done."

The hard tip of the cane tapped at her as he waited. Finally, she managed to lock her knees again, her fingernails digging into her forearm.

Three more strokes followed in quick succession, and this time, she screamed through clenched teeth, pain spiraling higher.

"Just a few more, then we're done, Ms. Hart."

Done? Already?

The prospect that this might be all he wanted buoyed her, even though she knew it was too good to be true.

Another cut burned across her ass, even lower, right at the join between buttock and thigh. She sprang up, clutching her swollen, weal-striped cheeks.

"I can't! God, you're killing me!" Tears streamed down her cheeks now.

"You're doing just fine." The cane tapped the desktop next to her. "Two more. Obey and I'll make them quick."

"I *can't*, Sir." She wiped tears from cheeks sticky with running mascara.

"Either you can, or you're backing out on the deal, Ms. Hart."

Just fucking do this, Alyson. You've got no choice.

She lowered herself once more, grasping the far edge of the desktop in a death grip, holding her breath.

"Good," he said, pleasure in his voice.

With two snaps, the last strokes whipped in, every bit as painful as the previous eight. She tensed against the desk, grunting as the pain bloomed, white-hot, then fading to a dull, persistent burning suffusing every inch of her ass. The heat had spread to more than just her buttocks, though, the realization a shock to her.

Yes, she'd fantasized about being spanked, whipped, dominated.

But that's all they were—fantasies.

The reality was much more painful than she'd imagined...though to a certain part of her body, that pain didn't seem to matter. She tightened her thighs together, clenching her stinging buttocks. With luck he wouldn't be able to see the evidence of her body's betrayal.

His low laughter made her want to turn around and slap him.

"You did well, Ms. Hart." A hand rucked up the thin fabric of her shirt, the warm palm stroking her bare skin. "I wasn't sure you'd actually go through with it. A thief you may be, but you're a courageous one too."

That big hand moved lower, stroking over the inflamed, throbbing weals, and she yelped, clenching her teeth. Fingers whispered at the lips of her sex.

She whimpered, pressing her face deeper into her arms as his fingers splayed her labia apart, exposing the sticky wetness within to the cool air.

"I thought so," he murmured.

Why was this happening? How was it even possible

her body had betrayed her like this?

His palm patted her swollen pussy with surprising gentleness, and his hands moved back up to her buttocks, caressing the curves of her hips.

"You need something for these. Stay there."

Moving around the desk once more, he slipped the cane back into its drawer. Incredibly, he began a soft whistling as he searched another drawer. The man was perfectly at ease! As if this were a mere afternoon's diversion.

"There we are," he said, pulling a round, silver tin from a drawer, then moving back behind her.

"Oh God," she gasped as the freezing cream was spread over her welts, his strong fingers kneading it into her aching buttocks, awakening yet more throbbing. "That hurts! Stop, please!"

"You're going to thank me for this later on tonight." He sat down on the desk next to her, his hand giving her ass a gentle pat. She moved to rise, but his hand fisted in her hair, pushing her head back down, her tear-soaked cheek pressed to her arms. "Stay where you are; the cream needs time to absorb. And there's something you need to hear."

Alyson tried not to think about how she must look, bent over a desk as if she were inviting him to fuck her, bare ass crisscrossed with swollen, aching weals.

Better this than a prison jumpsuit.

"Are you listening to me, Ms. Hart?" His hand clasped her hip, squeezing.

"Sorry, sir."

"This isn't over. You did well today, but you haven't satisfied your obligation to me. You owe me a month for what? Every thousand dollars you stole?"

Seven months of this? Oh God...

He continued, his thumb stroking possessive circles on her hip. "As of today, I own this very pretty ass of yours—and I intend to enjoy it. Whenever I call for you, you'll come to me. Whatever you're told to do, you'll do. Very simple, yet so very hard for a girl like you. Remember this, and you'll avoid a jail cell."

"Sir, I..."

"I'll allow you one question, Ms. Hart; then I want you to get your things and go home."

"What happens, at the end of this?"

"Your obligation will be fulfilled." He gave a harsh slap to her inflamed buttocks, making her grunt. "Now go home. Karen will have new job duties for you on Monday. Don't be late."

"Yes, sir." She'd rather die than be late and risk more of what had her ass throbbing angrily.

As she opened the front door, he stopped her.

"Ms. Hart. One more thing."

"Sir?" She lowered her head, not even looking back at him.

"What's your son's name?"

✧ ✧ ✧

HE WASTED NO time.

From a new desk—one he could easily walk past, to

and from his office—to a new job description, to new demands for her to start dressing to his specifications, he began tightening the noose immediately.

She'd wondered why he hadn't touched her sexually since that first caning—and she didn't want to contemplate why the thought seemed to haunt her every waking moment. Then came her second summons to his office for a lunch "meeting"—exactly two months since she'd agreed to his little…arrangement. But rather than another one of his searing punishments, he had other ideas.

As she'd knelt in that locked sun-soaked office, looking up at those intense blue eyes, she bared her breasts for him at his barked command. As he'd berated her for her shitty job performance, his heavy cock rearing over her waiting lips, it was the first time she'd stopped railing against the unfairness of it all but rather wondered what that cock would feel like on her tongue, how much she'd reluctantly begun to respond to it.

Sure, she still knew it was wrong, but she knew then that she could go the distance.

At first, it was mostly her days ruled by her tormentor in CEO's clothing, with more than one walk of shame from his office in the prescribed slutty heels, her pussy throbbing, his seed seeping down her leg.

But occasionally he'd wanted more than her days, and Will took care of that little problem too, sitting impatiently while Alyson interviewed—and instantly fell in love with—Maria, the rosy-cheeked nanny with the warm smile, the same woman who'd raised Will's own nephew.

More than a few late nights saw Alyson kissing the sleeping Noah good night while Maria let herself out quietly. Alyson would sit in the dark next to her beautiful blond-haired boy, listening to him softly snore, the clamps under her blouse tormenting her, her nipples going from a throbbing to numbness—one of the myriad little punishments Will enjoyed inflicting, relishing the knowledge that he could discipline her even from afar.

By degrees, her world became his. She'd bend for him in his office for short, sharp appointments with his hand, followed by the hard pounding of her pussy over his creaking desk, his fist twisted in her hair. A Saturday summons to his home for reviewing reports, a whipping for her soft, swinging breasts, and riding him, his big cock forcing yet more dark, humiliating climaxes from her bound, blindfolded, and gagged form. She'd long ago given up the idea of disobeying his dictates—and he knew it—and as the days wore on, that fact worried her even more than the warring of fear and twisted, confusing anticipation that crept into her mind each time he called her to one of his little "appointments."

By dint of agonizing discipline, his slave-driving work ethic, and a sexual use of her that had reduced her to little more than a play toy for his lusts, a change had been wrought in her. No longer was she ever late. Her mind, if not her conscience, was clear. Her work improved. She was able to be fully present with Noah, focused on her beloved son, enjoying each moment with him, knowing how precious and wonderful even a moment's peace had become to her.

It was the most difficult when she'd seen that faraway look in Will's eyes, that look he took great pains to hide from her but hadn't always succeeded. When he was kind rather than cruel. When he held her, stroking her hair while she sobbed against his chest, his caresses soft after a harsh spanking. And when he allowed her into his bed, her heart twisting as he curled around her, his arms gathering her close in his slumber, his breath gentle against her hair as, over and over, he whispered her name.

The day came where Alyson worried less about how many days were left in her sentence, and instead thought of what might come afterward.

And wondered whether anything *should* come afterward.

✧ ✧ ✧

7 months later

HE WOULD BE there any minute, and she'd be in deep shit if she wasn't ready. As she always did while waiting for him, she went over The Rules:

> *1. You will be on your knees, facing the door, when I arrive home. You'll be naked and bound.*

She'd made her way into his bedroom—he'd given

her his key after the first month—then she'd knelt on the thick gray carpet. It was always a moment of panic before she cinched that last cuff, the steel cold against her wrists. The manacles attached to thick leather thigh cuffs, keeping her hands out of the way, her breasts utterly defenseless. The scent of his body permeated the room. She'd hated it once, the scent of the one who tormented her.

But she didn't hate it anymore.

2. You will obey any instruction I give you. No exceptions.

It had started that first day at work. He'd actually sent her an e-mail:

"Go to the restroom, take off your panties and bra and send them to my office via interoffice memo envelope."

Alyson remembered reading it several times in disbelief. She'd known she should've taken that e-mail, and the countless other instances of correspondence, and gone to the police. Sure, she'd go to jail, but she'd take him down too.

But still she hadn't done it—and it took her seven months to be able to admit the reason why.

3. You will not protest, save crying out or screaming—unless you've decided not to honor your obligation.

The thick steel rings still made her nipples tingle as she knelt in the cool, quiet bedroom. She hadn't even cried out when they'd been done, quiet tears wetting the hair at her temples. He'd told her to have her nipples pierced, and she'd obeyed. Simple as that.

Her life had become his rules, his demands, his lusts. And her job was to submit herself to all of them.

His bedroom door opened, then closed, the air currents moving over her naked body. Her gaze fixated on the pattern of the carpet, not daring to meet his eyes until he gave her leave to do so. The gleaming black of his Guccis stopped before her. He tested her hard nipples, pinching, elongating them, lifting the rings on his fingertips a moment, his pleased murmur making her blush. Then he unlocked her cuffs, and his hand tapped her thigh.

"Up on the bed. Tits on the mattress, ass up."

Scrambling to obey, she rested her cheek on her arms, the cold metal of her nipple rings pressed against her flesh. His thick cock slid into her, and she sighed as his hands took firm hold of her hips.

"I thought about this cunt at the shareholders' meeting today. Thought of you waiting here for me, on your knees. Obedient." His palm slapped her ass hard, and she hissed with the sting. "Squeeze. That's a girl."

He took up a hard, punishing thrusting. Her aching nipples rasped against the comforter. He gathered up her arms, holding her wrists in his hand at her back, using them as leverage to thrust yet deeper, the hard head battering her cervix with a confusing pleasure/pain on each strong plunge. She moaned as he slapped her bottom once more, the heat flaring, her pussy clenching in sympathy around the mercilessly thrusting cock.

"Don't come; don't you dare," he rumbled behind her, his big hand pinning her to the mattress. With a groan he bucked against her, the springs of the mattress whispering in time with the heavy thrusts. Pressing close, he held himself deep, Alyson gasping, the hot seed blooming within her. Her clit throbbed, as bereft of his touch as the impossibly hard points of her nipples.

Her hips rotated against him, a slight movement, but one she knew he prohibited. A hard slap to her ass followed, his voice a warning growl. She murmured disappointment as he pulled himself from her.

"On your back, girl. Up to the headboard, arms back."

His strong arms helped slide her up, locking her wrists in the familiar leather cuffs, the blindfold shutting out all light as he cinched it tight behind her head. His hands urged her legs apart.

"Open." He slapped her thigh, the bright flash of pain making her squeak. "Come on, farther. That's good."

The muscles of her inner thighs ached, stretched wide, her shaved, splayed pussy dripping with his semen, embarrassingly wet, the scent of sex heavy in the air. With her sight denied her, she was at once eager and fearful of what he had planned for her next.

The rough pad of his thumb slicked back the hood of her clit, the calloused digit working it almost painfully as she panted.

"Look at this poor little pussy, come dripping from it," he said, his tone rich with pleasure. Her sex was stroked, the outer labia pinched and massaged between knowing fingertips. Then a broad, wet tongue rasped over her exposed clit, and she arched up with a harsh intake of breath, her thighs rigid.

"Oh God, please…"

"Be still. If you're good, you might get what you need."

An orgasm? My freedom? Your affection?

Fingers slid inside her wetness, curling, making her groan. He'd never touched her like this before, yet he knew exactly where, how to touch her. The pleasure built as he stroked her with one, then two fingers, occasionally licking her hard, throbbing clit with the rasp of his tongue.

"You're going to come for me, girl. I want to see you squirt all over my fingers." The mattress dipped to one side, his forearm against her rib cage. His lips took hers then, at first softly tasting, exploring, then hard, his tongue driving deep, claiming. "So helpless, girl. Mine." His lips brushed against her cheek, breath warm on her skin. "Are you mine, my little thief?"

The words were on her tongue, confusion, fear, and a new unsettling elation warring within her. What did it mean that she wanted him to take her, that she wanted to feel those soft possessive lips upon hers once more? To kiss him forever, until she could forget what she'd done, could accept what he'd done, what had led them to this day.

"I need…" This was more than she could cope with, these emotions welling up within her, the power of them so unexpected, so shattering. This was much more than survival, than penance, than duty, more even than lust.

His fingers slipped inside her once more, his thumb circling her clit as he worked that spot within her until she moaned.

"Come for me, girl. Show me. You've got no choice." His lips sucked her clit into his mouth, her moans vibrating through her whole body as she arched up. Fingers worked her harder, her hips writhing as he thrust within her drenched sex, the coppery smell of his semen mixing with the thick scent of her own arousal.

"Oh *fuck*."

"That's it. Be a good girl. Surrender to it. Surrender to *me*."

Another devastating curl of his fingers and she was panting, pulling at the tight bonds holding her wrists, her heels beating upon the mattress.

"Please, sir! *Please…*"

"Come now, Alyson."

She screamed, the heavy feeling coming deep within, and the familiar split second of panic that she might pee all over his bed. She squeezed down upon those fingers, and her pussy gushed, soaking her thighs and his hand in her juices, her loud moans almost pained, her abdomen clenching tight, over and over.

"Oh good, *so* good," he said, his voice thick with lust. "I want more, girl. More!"

His thumb rasped her clit, and she went over, every nerve ending firing at once, all sound, all sight, all awareness leaving her in a white-hot burst of pleasure.

He kept working her gently, silently, those fingers knowing just what she needed and what she feared, playing with her too-sensitive clit, stroking the swollen, burning lips of her sex. He kissed her inner thighs, the stubble at his chin rough against her tender skin.

"Sir, please. I can't. Not anymore, *please.*"

"Shh now." He released her arms, his body sliding up between her legs. She murmured as the hot weight of his erection rested across her inner thigh. Then his thumbs eased her open, the broad head of his cock seeking the entrance, sinking slowly within her, every inch of him reawakening nerve endings as he stretched her. His cock fully seated within her, his fingers removed the blindfold, and he loomed above her, the deep blue eyes so close, intent, fathomless.

Beautiful.

She closed her eyes against it, her emotions raw. She should hate this man, despise him for what he'd wrought upon her. But as her pussy drew him deeper, her arms around him, her heels crossing at the rise of his strong buttocks, she knew the awful, bittersweet truth of things.

And it was something that could never be.

"Look at me," he said, his voice ragged. "I want to see your eyes."

Her gaze met his, and he took her then, savagely, that fiery blue gaze pinning her beneath him as surely as his thick, thrusting cock had. He didn't speak a word, his jaws clenched, sweat gathering at his upper lip, his veined, muscled arms surrounding her, his breath coming in quickening grunts.

A single tear escaped and ran down her temple as she looked up at him, her sex clenching upon him, a last long moan rising in her throat as his thrusts rose to a punishing, fevered pitch. He fell upon her as he came again, his powerful body freezing, then pounding against hers as he groaned his pleasure.

Finally he stilled, his heavy body a pleasing weight upon her own, and she stared up at the ceiling, his lips moving against her neck, whispering one word:

"Alyson."

They lay together then, his hand stroking the mess of her hair, her body curved over his, neither saying a word in the quiet, dark night.

And as Alyson feared what would come, what *had* to come next, sleep finally claimed her.

✧ ✧ ✧

SHE FOUND HIS card on her keyboard at work the next day. On it were written four simple words:

"Last day. Obligation fulfilled."

She walked down to his office, thinking of the times she'd made that same walk with her heart in her throat. Now, she made it with tears in her eyes. But Karen's sympathetic smile told Alyson what she already knew.

He was gone.

It was Christmas Eve, and Connie let her go home early to hug Noah, to never let him go, to whisper in his ear as he giggled that she'd always love him, that he'd always be her little man.

Christmas morning, as she sat snuggled on her couch, her cup of coffee warming her palm if not her spirits, she watched Noah dive into his presents, helped by Alyson's mother and, at Noah's insistence, Maria too.

As Alyson tried to push the thoughts of Will away, bury them for good, Noah jumped into her lap.

"Whoa, tiger, you're gonna spill Mama's coffee!" She pecked him on the nose, and he smiled, his brilliant green eyes sparkling.

"You missed one, Mommy."

The white envelope was pressed into her hand, and he laid a wet little-boy kiss on her cheek, bounding off to play with his new toys.

She tore it open, the outside of the card showing a picture of two silver interlocked rings. Inside, written in the familiar spare script, were five simple words, and as she read them, tears streamed down Alyson's face.

"First day. Obligation never fulfilled."

ACQUITTED
GISELLE RENARDE

"I CAN'T BELIEVE I raised such a naive daughter."

Her mother set down the knife and said, "You really think he's innocent, don't you?"

Lucy's spine straightened vertebra by vertebra against the wooden chair rail. "Me and twelve members of the jury."

"She doesn't just *think* he's innocent," Caroline said, clasping Lucy's hand. "Sean *is* innocent."

"Thank you, Caroline." Lucy glared across the kitchen. "It's nice to have somebody's support in this family."

Their mother went on chopping carrots and said nothing.

"People like you don't even care about the truth. You just believe what you want to believe." Lucy started feeling itchy all over. That was her body's new reaction to this interminable argument—burning up from the inside out. "Can you even imagine how it would impact your life, being wrongly accused?"

"And of *murder*," Caroline said softly. She didn't mention the rape charge, but that was just as well.

The kitchen filled with the metronomic sound of Mom slicing carrots, smashing her knife against the cutting board like she had a bone to pick with that block of wood.

Lucy's blood boiled. What was point? She'd tried; she'd failed. Grabbing her purse, she said, "I can't take any more of your judgmental bullshit. I'm outta here."

Her mother slammed down the knife as Caroline pleaded, "Don't go. At least stay for dinner."

"I'm making your favorite," Mom said.

"Yeah, well I never asked you to," Lucy shot back. "The only thing I ever asked was for you to be nice to the man I love. Why can't you treat him like a human being?"

"Because," her mother shouted. "There's something off about that boy. You're still young, Lucy. You don't see it. You don't understand that charming isn't the same as good. In fact, the charmers are the ones you have to watch out for."

"Yeah right, Mom. You would know." Lucy looked to her sister for back-up, but Caroline's mouth hung mutely open. "Just because you have lousy taste in men doesn't mean I do."

Lucy didn't stick around for the retort. She stamped out the door, slamming it behind her just like she used to as a teenager. It bugged the hell out of her that her own mother couldn't be supportive of her relationship. What was the point in hating all her boyfriends? It only made Lucy cling to them tighter.

Mothers didn't understand anything.

When she got home, Sean looked up from the TV. "Hey, I thought you were eating at your mom's house."

"No," Lucy grumbled.

Sean turned off the television and rose from the couch. "Hey, hey now... why the long face?"

Lucy shook her head. "It's nothing."

"It's something, I bet." He wrapped his arms around her, and as soon as the warmth of his skin played off hers, she lost it. "Tell me all about it, babe. Tell me what's wrong."

She soaked his top with tears as she stammered, "She always does this, every time I love someone, but it's worse with you. She thinks you did it."

"And that makes you wonder if I did?"

"No!" Lucy pulled back so she could look him in the eye. "Sean, no, never. If I thought for a second that you did it, would I even be here right now? Would I have let you move in with me?"

"I don't know," he said, with what might have been a smirk on his lips.

She whacked him on the shoulder. "Come on, dude, you know I have faith in you."

"Oh, yeah?" He wove his arms around her body, hugging her forcefully enough that breath fled her lungs. "It's too bad you're the only one."

"I'm not," Lucy told him. "Caroline believes you, too. It's just my mom who's closed-minded about all this stuff. She can't set aside the accusation and see the acquittal."

When he let go of her, air surged into her lungs so hard it hurt. He surprised her by saying, "Don't worry what your mother thinks."

"Why wouldn't I?" Lucy asked. "My mom thinks you're a murderer. Doesn't that bother you?"

"Nope." Sitting on the arm of the couch, he drew her playfully into his lap.

As he bounced her on his knee, she couldn't help laughing. "Stop it, Sean! Can't you be serious for a second?"

"I've been serious for many, many seconds—minutes, even. Hours at a time!" He nuzzled her neck. "Serious is highly overrated."

She had to respect his wishes. After all, he'd been forced to spend time in jail, awaiting a trial for things he didn't do. The whole country was still convinced he'd killed that woman, raped her too. Who was Lucy to tell him how he should feel?

"I love your neck," he said as he planted baby kisses all the way to her jawline. "Right here. This spot."

The way his lips warmed her flesh sparked a tingle in her core. His hand followed that tingle, resting on her belly gently and then moving in slow circles, lower, parting her thighs enough to rub between them. She swelled for him as his mouth found hers. God, was his tongue ever strong. Every time he kissed her, she felt his tongue like a ghost against her clit. It was just her imagination, she knew, but the sensation was so realistic that her jeans suddenly felt two sizes too small.

"Come on, babe." She slid out of his lap, tugging him toward the bedroom. "I'll strip for you."

"Oh, you think so?" He darted up from the couch and, coming in behind her, wrapped his prison-sculpted arms around her neck.

"Sean…" It was a variation on a hug. Sometimes he didn't realize his own strength, didn't seem to sense that his grip was too tight. "Let go. I can't breathe."

"I know you can't." His voice was a seductive growl, like he wanted her to acknowledge that his love exerted total power over her. "Don't you like it?"

"No." It hurt. She tried to swallow, but she couldn't. "Stop."

All at once, he let go. Just like that. Easy.

When Lucy touched the sensitive place where his arms had been, Sean laughed. "Let's go out for a bit."

Dazed, she asked, "Out where? Should I change?"

"Nah," he said and then swiftly changed his tune. "Actually, yeah. Put on that dress I like."

He didn't have to explain. She knew exactly which one he meant, and closed the bedroom door as she slipped out of her jeans. Christ, were her panties ever slick! He'd really turned her on just then. Was it the kissing or the roughhousing? Her mom would read too much into the way he'd grabbed her just then, taking her neck too tightly in his arms. The truth was that every guy she'd been with had enjoyed the rough stuff. Her mind didn't want to want it, but her body knew better.

Lucy slipped her gauzy summer dress over her head and tied the halter around the back of her neck. She couldn't feel his touch anymore, and she missed it. Where was he taking her? Hopefully somewhere they could sneak away for a naughty moment alone.

She never wore a bra with this dress, but the top part was fitted enough to keep her small breasts in check. If she didn't put on panties, would anyone be able to make out the curly orange wisps of her pubic hair? She tried out every angle in front of the mirror and finally decided she didn't care whether people could see through the fabric. She'd be on Sean's arm. She'd dress for him alone.

"No heels," he said through the door. "Flats."

Lucy kicked off the shoes she'd just slid her feet into, and put on ballet flats instead. Very cute.

"Okay, I'm ready." She threw open the door and paraded down the hall like it was her own personal runway. "Tell me what you think."

The gleam in his eyes said it all, but he didn't stop there. Grabbing her wrist, he pulled her into his arms, crushing her small body to his chest. He kissed again, more forcefully than before, running one hand down her ass and squeezing.

"You're wearing a thong," he growled, his breath hot on her ear.

"No." She pulled up on her cotton skirt. "I'm not."

She held his sizzling gaze as he swooped his hand

around the base of her bum. His fingers teased her flesh as she parted her legs, just slightly, for him. The moment he dabbed into her wetness, his eyes lit up. She could taste his hunger.

"Bad girl," he said in a way Lucy couldn't quite read. Was he aroused or angry? That expression could have gone either way.

He answered her silent question with a smack.

Lucy's spine straightened. Her heart raced. She heard the spanking land before she actually felt it, and for a moment she thought perhaps she'd get off easy—maybe she wouldn't feel the burn at all.

No such luck. After a lost moment, a palm-shaped blaze flashed across her skin. Warmth, not pain. The *next* one brought pain. It came so out of the blue that she threw herself against his strong chest, like he could save her from himself.

But he couldn't. He didn't. He smacked her again, sending a shock of pain beyond her flesh. His spanking hurt so hard she felt it in her blood.

"Put on some panties." He found her hips with both hands and pushed her toward the bedroom. "Cotton ones. The tiny cotton panties with the lace around the edges."

Was she blushing? Spankings always did that to her.

Nodding, she stepped backward into the bedroom. She couldn't take her eyes off his. God, that stare—when he looked at her that way, she felt owned. She felt special. She was the only one who truly believed in him, and he knew that. He knew how much she loved him, because he loved her every bit as much. They were made for each other.

She was just stepping into her panties when he opened the front door. "Get a move on, Lucy. Only a few more hours of daylight."

Tripping over her feet, she grabbed her purse and a light pashmina. "Coming! Don't leave home without me."

"Like I could *live* without you." He snuck his arm around her neck as she locked the door, creating a playful triangle, his elbow just below her chin. "I couldn't, you know."

"I know." She ducked before he could tighten his grip, slipping away from him like a ghost, giggling as she raced toward the elevator. "Ha! I escaped."

"Get back here, you." He ran after her, grasping her waist and lifting her off her feet before she could press the button. "You can never escape. I'm always gonna be here."

"Good." A giddy tingle sparkled through her body as he turned her in his arms. "I want you forever."

His lips found hers as the elevator door squealed open. As he carried her across the threshold, she didn't stop kissing him even long enough to check if anyone was staring at them. There mustn't have been, because Sean wouldn't dip his strong hands under her skirt in front of witnesses…would he?

"God, I'm so turned on." He broke their kiss to set

her down as the empty elevator opened. "You don't know what you do to me."

"I think I do," she countered. "Wanna fuck in the car? Wouldn't that be dirty?"

"We're not taking the car." He swept her from the lobby. Instead of heading out front, they went the back way. "We're going for a long walk."

"Oh." She did her best to conceal her disappointment.

Why did he ask her to put on a dress if they were just going for a walk? And he knew she'd passed up dinner at her mother's house—couldn't he anticipate that she might be hungry? *Starving?*

But one look at that chiseled jaw, that sparkling white smile, and she couldn't stay mad. "Whatever you want, babe."

He escorted her toward the ravine path where neighbors jogged and walked their dogs. Hand in hand, they walked until the dense forest opened into a clearing. She hadn't worn her watch, so it was hard to say how long they'd been at it. His company was magic. She could listen to him for hours and never get bored.

"Where are we?" Lucy asked when the land took on a familiar tone, like a dreamscape or a childhood memory. "I think I've been here before, but…I don't know."

"There it is!" Pointing to a parking lot in the distance, Sean said, "Best chip truck in the country, I swear. Just wait till you taste their haddock. You'll be hooked."

Fish? From a truck? Lucy's instinct was to run far, far away, but it was actually sort of sweet that Sean had brought her on this wild-goose chase for fish and chips. And, once they'd lined up and ordered and found a cozy picnic table where they could eat, she found that he was right. "Wow, these really are the best chips I've ever tasted."

"Try the fish," he said, breaking through the deep-fried batter with his plastic fork. "It's better than sex."

Lucy raised an eyebrow. "Like that could even be possible."

Her first bite was so hot she had to suck in air to cool her palate. After a sip of water and another go, the sweet filet filled her mouth with such a succulent flavor that she didn't even care that her calf muscles were twitching and blisters threatened her big toes.

"You're right," she said. "This fish is better than sex."

They smiled at each other as they chewed, because sometimes just being together was the greatest joy in the entire world. But when Lucy teased a French fry in ketchup and Sean didn't react, she followed his blank stare and asked, "What?"

"Those guys." He offered a subtle nod. "They're talking about me."

"How can you tell?"

"I just can."

Lucy had been in this situation enough to know

how to conduct herself. As three large men approached their picnic table, she dug into the fish, trying to ignore the shiver down her spine.

"Hey! You!" The men were older, maybe in their fifties, but Lucy felt intimidated by their sheer size. "Are you Sean Scott?"

Sean looked around. "Who, me?"

"Yeah you. Who d'you think I'm talking to?"

"I... I don't know," Sean stammered. He was getting good at pretending he wasn't himself.

The first time this happened, Lucy was dumb enough to stand up for Sean. It had been girls that time—probably in their teens—but Lucy had picked a fight, thinking she'd win. She'd shouted about how Sean had been acquitted, which meant he wasn't guilty, which meant everybody just had to leave the poor guy alone.

She wouldn't try that again.

"Sean Scott—the guy who killed that girl down by the lake?" The men seemed much less certain than they had.

"Yeah, I know who you're talking about, but I'm not him."

The biggest man traced his hand down a salt-and-pepper beard and said, "You look just like the guy."

"I don't think that's a compliment," Sean said.

Lucy smiled, but she was suddenly having trouble with the charade.

"So you're not him?" asked the man in a torn T-shirt and sweat pants.

Sean shook his head. "I'm not him."

"Oh." All three men bowed their heads slightly, like that way the only way they knew to offer an apology, and then tramped toward the chip truck.

Digging her fork into the fish, Lucy focused on the crisp crackle of batter and the little shoot of steam that rose from the filet. She didn't look Sean in the eye. She couldn't.

"Look at them, skulking away with their tails between their legs." Sean chuckled as he dipped his chips in ketchup.

"This is the park, isn't it?" Swallowing past the lump in her throat, Lucy asked, "This is the place where the body was found."

"Yup," Sean replied, like it was no big deal. "In the lake down that path over there. Not out in the open or anything. It's a remote spot."

Lucy's throat burned. She couldn't eat any more. "I don't like that you know so much about it."

"Why?" His tone remained jovial, but she still couldn't bring herself to look at his face. "I sat in that courtroom while the Crown dug into every little detail, went through every morsel of evidence for the jury. Trust me—I paid close attention."

All at once, the tension fell out of Lucy's shoulders. "Jesus, I'm sorry, Sean. I didn't even think."

"It's okay, babe." When he reached for her hand, she gazed into his calm, caring eyes and felt like an idiot for doubting him.

"No, it's not okay. You said yourself I'm the only person in the world you can count on. Who does it help when I question you?"

"It's fine." His grip tightened around her hand. "Honestly."

Her mouth watered, but the tender fish didn't hit the spot, no matter how much she ate. Neither did the fries.

"I can take you there, if you want to see it."

Lucy's stomach tightened while her thighs warmed. "Take me…?"

"Where they found the body," Sean said.

"You know where they found it? How?" She didn't want to know.

Scooping up their garbage, Sean rose from the picnic table. "Like I said—they went over all this stuff, in detail, during my trial. Did you follow it on the news or anything?"

"No," Lucy said, but that was a lie.

"Oh, they grilled me on the stand, especially about how my semen got into her body." He dumped their trash in a bin and then took Lucy by the hand, leading her toward the path. "Those lawyers, I tell you, they didn't want to believe the sex was consensual. Tamryn and I came here on a date—that's why so many witnesses reported seeing us."

"Oh. Okay." Lucy wished he would stop speaking, but she couldn't ask him to stifle himself. Who else could he talk to, if not her?

"She had a thing for sex in public, sex in the woods. I'd never done anything so daring, but she loved it and we hadn't been dating very long so I didn't want to seem like a prude."

Lucy laughed. "You? A prude?"

"Not anymore." As they dipped into a private nook of trees, Sean's hand found its way to Lucy's thigh, then slipped up her skirt, cupping her bum. "God, I love this ass."

"How much?" she asked as he pressed her up against a tree.

His mouth found hers as he squeezed her bum with both hands. It wasn't enough just to touch her over her cotton panties. He dug inside, touching her skin, treating it roughly, just the way she liked. Her pussy pulsed with every squeeze. She almost wished he'd take her over his knee, but this was hardly the place for a spanking. Too public. People might hear when she cried out in pain.

"I fucked Tamryn up against this tree."

He pressed his hardness against her belly, but she didn't react. When he kissed her this time, she didn't kiss him back.

"What's wrong?" he asked.

"Nothing." Lucy plastered on a smile. "It's fine."

"Obviously not." His hands found hers. "You don't like me talking about it?"

"I'm sorry." She fell into his arms, hugging him

sweetly. "I'm an idiot. How stupid is it to be jealous?"

Sean crushed her to his chest. "Jealous of a dead girl?"

Lucy didn't answer. It was getting hard to breathe.

"Don't be." He kissed her hair, then let go.

The summer breeze rushed into her lungs. She couldn't get enough of that sensation: the inability to function, the waiting to see when he'd give her life, and then the sudden return from the borders of death.

"Come over here." He took her hand and led her off the beaten track, down an incline that was slippery with pine needles, and then to a rocky terrain by the water.

Gravel-sized rock shards ran like spikes through the soles of Lucy's ballet slippers. Her feet were killing her, but she didn't complain. Her pain was nothing important.

"It was early afternoon, still nice and bright when she brought out her watercolor pad and paint pots. She liked this spot, for the sparkle of the sun off the lake, and the landscape across the way. She used lake water to paint. I thought that was really cute."

"Yeah." Lucy nodded. "It is."

"I wanted to watch, but that made her nervous. She could only paint alone. No biggie. She stayed and I left. And that was the last time I ever saw her."

"Alive," Lucy added, though, Christ, what a stupid thing to say. "Sorry."

Gazing across the lake, Sean stretched his arm around Lucy's shoulder. "They found her faceup, right over here."

When he walked, she went with him. What else could she do? She was trapped against his body. Also, though she didn't want to admit it even to herself, her body began to tingle when he talked about the crime.

"They thought you murdered her in the water," Lucy said. "Strangled her with your bare hands."

"On the shoreline." He led her there. "Where the rock gives way to sand. Just this little patch here. The area isn't visible from the path. I guess people standing on the opposite shoreline could see way over here, but the murderer would only be a speck. They'd need binoculars to see him properly."

"They're sure it was a man?" Lucy asked.

"If it was a woman, she'd have to have some powerful grip and a hell of a weight on her. *You* couldn't have done this."

"I didn't know I was a suspect," she teased.

"I didn't know *I* was," Sean shot back. "Not at first. When the police asked me to help with their inquiries, I really thought that's what I was doing: helping. Can't believe how dumb I was."

"Well, why would you think you were a suspect? She was your girlfriend. You wouldn't think of killing her any more than you'd think to kill me."

Sean ran his fingers down her bare arm, and her skin tingled. Terrible timing, but she knew what she needed. When his hand approached hers, she grasped his wrist. Plunging his palm between her legs, she helped him rub there, slow but hard.

He didn't seem shocked. Not in the least. In fact, he tugged up her skirt, making it dance against her thighs, teasing her smooth skin.

"What was she wearing that day?" Lucy asked.

Sean gripped her pussy over the tight stretch of her panties, hugging it with his hand. The heat from his body filled her bones, soaring from her cunt to her skull, making her dizzy.

"A dress?" Her legs threatened to collapse beneath her as she stepped out of her ballet flats and into warm, wet sand. She grabbed him by the crotch and took him with her, until the lake lapped at their ankles. "Were her panties made of cotton?"

"Always," Sean groaned.

She unzipped his fly and found his cock, took it out, stroked it. Falling to her knees, Lucy asked, "Did Tamryn ever do this?"

Without waiting for an answer, she wrapped her lips around his tip. His precum drizzled across her tongue like frosting, and she swallowed it eagerly. He never answered her question, but maybe she didn't want an answer. Maybe she just wanted to feel his hands in her hair, gripping it tightly while she sucked.

Christ, did his cock ever feel good in her mouth. The perfect size, perfect girth—just enough to stretch her capacity without injuring the back of her throat. She threw her body into it, devouring his dick while she wrapped both hands around the base of his shaft.

"Oh, you can't..." He pushed her shoulders. "You can't. I'm gonna come."

"So come," she said around his cock.

"No." A deep growl emerged from the back of his throat as he pulled out of her mouth. "I gotta fuck you first."

Throwing her down in the sand, Sean got on top, trapping her half in, half out of the lake. Her dress soaked up water like a sponge as her bare feet sank below the surface. He straddled her with his dick surging out the front of his pants, and when she tried to grab it, he pinned her arms to the ground.

"No," he said. "Your hands are sandy."

"Oh." She laughed, but she was too stunned to say anything more.

"I need your pussy, babe."

"It's yours," Lucy said, keeping quiet, not wanting to get caught. "My panties are soaking wet."

"Your hot, tight, *soaking wet* pussy..." He let go of her arms to pull up her dress, then pressed his erection to the wet cotton. The heat from his dick passed right through the fabric, sizzling against the throbbing mass of her clit. Pressing his weight down, he crushed her into the sand while gentle waves licked their bodies. When he rocked on her, she felt his wild exuberance in every cell.

"I want you inside me," she said. They usually used condoms, but in that moment safety didn't seem important. "Fuck me, Sean. Fuck me like you fucked her."

Pressing his mouth to Lucy's ear, he said, "I told you—we fucked in the woods, up against the tree."

Lucy closed her eyes and pictured them from above. Was Tamryn watching? Hovering overhead as Sean shifted the gusset of Lucy's panties aside with his cock? What would the murdered girl think if she could see them now?

Her pussy was so wet it left a slick patch in the crotch of her underwear. Sean had no trouble pushing his cock inside her cunt, not satisfied to dabble in the shallows. He gave her pussy a few quick thrusts and then threw himself into the job, fucking her with wild abandon.

She closed her eyes and tried to exist as little as humanly possible. She breathed only when it was absolutely necessary, slow inhales and lengthy exhales. The lake had soaked through her entire dress now, and her nipples drew into tight buds, pressing through the fabric to prick Sean's chest. She didn't move her arms or her legs.

Playing dead altered her state of consciousness so drastically that the friction of his cock in her cunt got her hotter with every thrust. His chest sat on hers like a rock, like a weight, driving the breath from her lungs. Though she wasn't moving, her mind whirled. She felt dizzy enough to fall over, and she was already lying still.

It wasn't just Sean's motion that threw her senses into a tailspin. Tiny waves crashed like ocean tides against her bare skin. Birds in the trees sang at a hundred decibels. The squirrels stomped through the underbrush like elephants. Everything overwhelmed her, but nothing more so than Sean's hands as they looped around her throat.

"Tamryn," he moaned. "Who would do a thing like this? Wrap his hands around your little neck and tighten his grip? Strangle you until you were dead?"

Lucy wasn't sure if his grip was really as tight as it felt, or if her hyperbolizing imagination just experienced it that way. Her belly spun and tightened as he drove his cock again, again, again, grunting with every thrust. She felt like she'd just stepped off that twirly-whirly playground ride that had spun her in circles as a kid. That was her first memory of feeling any kind of arousal. *The twirly-whirlies.* That's what they'd called the sensation. Unoriginal but, to them, it represented joy and fear all wrapped into one.

Now Lucy had it bad. Her head felt loopy, though she hadn't moved in—how long? Time had fallen out of her grasp. Had they been fucking for minutes or hours? She had absolutely no idea.

"It hurts," she heard herself gasp.

Sean's thighs trembled against hers. His cock throbbed inside her cunt. He held his hands around her neck as her eyes rolled back. Light filled her mind as the late-afternoon sun gleamed off the lake. She'd never seen anything so beautiful, and her eyes weren't even open.

His hands fell away from her throat, but his weight

drove her deeper into the sand as his body relaxed. Prickly stubble dug into her cheek like razor blades. His breath came hot and fast, hers cold and slow. He'd gone in like a lion. She'd come out like a lamb. Her skin tingled, like tiny fairy feet were dancing all over it. Lake water had filled her pussy, but it rejected everything that wasn't Sean's cock—that still pulsed inside her flesh.

"You didn't make a sound," Sean said. "I thought you might..."

Lucy's mind worked slow as molasses, considering responses, rejecting them. She felt heavy and light, both at once. Part of her sank into the sand while another part rose to the heavens. She couldn't bring herself to speak.

But if she could, she'd have said to him, *This is the place where poor Tamryn was killed.* She'd have realized her mother knew a thing or two about character, and said, *I know how she felt when she died.*

Want more from Giselle Renarde? You can read MONSTROUS OBSESSION, a darkly demonic paranormal erotic romance.

Thank you!

Dear readers,

Thank you for reading *Take the Heat!*

The criminal mind has always fascinated me, so putting this anthology together has been amazing. You can help spread the word about Take the Heat by:

- Telling a friend about it! Word of mouth is the best way to share books.
- Leaving a review. Reviews help readers discover new books.

I love exploring dark impulses within the realm of romance, and I know my readers do too. That's why I'm so excited to share *Prisoner*, which was co-written with my friend and amazing author New York Times Bestseller Annika Martin. Turn the page for an excerpt…

Yours,
Skye Warren

Excerpt from Prisoner

HEAVY BARS CLOSE behind me with a clang. I feel the sound in my bones. A series of mechanical clicks hint at an elaborate security mechanism beneath the black iron plating. I knew this would happen—had anticipated and dreaded it—but my breathing quickens with the knowledge that I am well and truly trapped.

"Can I help you?"

I whirl to face the administrative window where a heavyset woman in a security guard uniform stares at her screen.

"Hi," I say, pasting on a smile. "My name is Abigail Winslow, and I'm here to—"

"Two forms of identification."

"Oh, well, I already filled out the paperwork at the front desk. And showed them my IDs."

"This isn't the front desk, Ms. Winslow. This is the east-wing desk, and I need to see two forms of identification."

"Right." I dig through my bag for my driver's license and passport.

She accepts them without looking up, then hands me a clipboard with a stack of papers just like the ones I already filled out.

I've been dreading this day for weeks, wishing I'd

been assigned any other project but this one. You'd think I was being sent here for a crime. My professor—the one who'd forced me into this—warned me that prisoners were not always receptive to outsiders. Apparently nobody here is.

I complete each form, arrange the pages neatly on the clipboard, and bring them back up to the window. The guard accepts them and gives back my IDs...still without looking at me.

My hands clench and unclench, clench and unclench while the guard eyes my paperwork.

Seconds pass. Or are they minutes? The damp chill of the place seeps in through my cardigan and leaves me shivering.

Leaning forward, I read the name tag of the guard. "Ms. Breck. Do you know what the next steps are?"

"You can have a seat. I have work to do now, and then I'll escort you back."

"Oh, okay." I glance at the bars I just came through, then the open hallway opposite. "Actually, if you just point me in the direction of the library, I'm sure I can—"

Thunk. The woman's hand hits the desk. I jump. Her dark eyes are faintly accusing, and I wish we could go back to no eye contact. How did I manage to make an enemy in two minutes?

"Ms. Winslow," she says, her voice patronizing.

"You can call me Abby," I whisper.

A slight smile. Not a nice one. "Ms. Winslow, what

do you think we do here?"

The question is clearly rhetorical. I press my lips together to keep from making things worse.

"The Kingman Correctional Facility houses over five thousand convicted criminals. My job is to keep it that way. Do we understand each other?"

Heat floods my cheeks. The last thing I want to do is make her job harder. "Right. Of course." I shamble back, landing hard on the metal folding chair. It wobbles a little before the rubber feet stop my slide.

I understand the woman's point. She has to keep the prisoners in and everyone else out, and keep people like me safe.

I reach down and pull a book from my bag. I never leave home without one, even when I go to classes or run errands. Even when I was young and my mother used to take me on her rounds.

Especially then.

I would hide in the backseat with my nose in the book, pretending I didn't see the shady people who came to her window when we stopped.

A little green light above the barred doors flashes on and there's an ominous buzz. Somebody's coming through, and I doubt it will be a library volunteer. I slide down.

Pretend to be invisible.

It's no use. I peer over the top edge as a prisoner saunters through the door, and my pulse slams in my throat double time.

He's flanked by two guards—escorted by them, I guess you'd say. But they seem more like an entourage than anything. Power vibrates around him like a threat.

Read, read, read. Don't look.

The prisoner is half a foot taller than the guards, but he seems to tower over them by more than that. Maybe it's his broad shoulders or just something about the way he stands, or his imperiously high cheekbones. The dark stubble across his cheeks looks so rough and unforgiving I can feel it against my palm; it contrasts wildly with the plushness of his lips. His short brown hair is mussed. There's one scar through his eyebrow that somehow adds to his perfection.

The little group approaches the window. I can barely breathe.

"ID number 85359," one of the guards says, and I understand that he's referring to the prisoner. That's who he is. Not John Smith or William Brown or whatever his name is. He's been reduced to a number. The woman at the desk runs through a series of questions. It's a procedure for checking him out of solitary.

The prisoner faces sideways, spine straight, the corner of his mouth tilted up as if he's slightly amused. Then it clicks, what else is so different about him: no visible tattoos. Tough guys like this, they're always inked up—it's a kind of armor, a kind of *fuck you*. This guy has none of it, though he's far from pristine; white scars mar the rough skin of his hands and especially his forearms, a latticework of pain and violence, a flag proclaiming the kind of underworld he came from.

The feel of brutality that hangs about him is compelling and...somehow beautiful.

I drink him in from behind my book—it's my mask, my protective shield. But then the strangest thing happens: he cocks his head. It's just a slight shift, but I feel his attention on me deep in my belly. I've been discovered. Caught by searchlights. Exposed.

My heart beats frantically.

I want him to look away. He fills up too much space. It's as if he breathes enough oxygen for twelve men, leaving no air for me at all. Maybe if we were in the library and he needed help finding a book or looking something up, then I wouldn't mind the weight of his attention.

No. Not even there. He's too much.

Two sets of bars on the gate. Handcuffs. Two guards.

What do they think he would do if there were only one set of bars, one guard?

My blood races as the guards draw him away from the window and toward the inner door, toward where I sit. His heat pierces the chill around me as he nears. His deep brown eyes never once meet mine, but I have the sense of him looming over me as he passes, like a tree with a massive canopy. He continues on, two hundred pounds of masculine danger wrapped in all that beauty.

Even in chains, he seems vibrant, wild and free, a

force of nature—it makes me feel like I'm the one in prison. Safe. Small. Carefully locked down.

How would it feel to be that free?

"Ms. Winslow. *Ms. Winslow.*"

I jump, surprised to hear that the woman has been calling my name. "I'm sorry," I say as a strange sensation tickles the back of my neck.

The woman stands and begins pulling on her jacket. "I'll take you to the library now."

"Oh, that's great."

That shivery sensation gets stronger. Against my better judgment, I look down the hallway where the guards and the prisoner are walking off as one—a column of orange flanked by two thinner, shorter posts.

The prisoner glances over his shoulder. His mocking brown gaze searches me out, pins me with a subtle threat. Though it isn't his eyes that scare me. It's his lips—those beautiful, generous lips forming words that make my blood race.

Ms. Winslow.

No sound comes out, but I feel as though he's whispered my name right into my ear. Then he turns and strolls off.

Want to read more? Prisoner is available at Amazon.com, BarnesAndNoble.com, and iBooks..

BOOKS BY SKYE WARREN

Wanderlust
On the Way Home
Hear Me
Prisoner

Dark Nights Series
Keep Me Safe (prequel)
Trust in Me
Don't Let Go

The Beauty Series
Beauty Touched the Beast
Beneath the Beauty
Broken Beauty
Beauty Becomes You
The Beauty Series Compilation

Standalone Erotic Romance
His for Christmas
Take the Heat: A Criminal Romance Anthology
Sweetest Mistress
Below the Belt

Dystopia Series
Leashed
Caged

Author Bios

Skye Warren

The Magnolia Hotel

Skye Warren is the New York Times and USA Today Bestselling author of dark romantic fiction. Her books are raw, sexual and perversely romantic.

Pam Godwin

Unlawful Seduction

New York Times and USA Today Bestselling author, Pam Godwin, lives in the Midwest with her husband, their two children, and a foulmouthed parrot. When she ran away, she traveled fourteen countries across five continents, attended three universities, and married the vocalist of her favorite rock band.

Java, tobacco, and dark romance novels are her favorite indulgences, and might be considered more unhealthy than her aversion to sleeping, eating meat, and dolls with blinking eyes.

CYNTHIA RAYNE

Captivated

Cynthia Rayne is the Amazon best-selling author of the Four Horsemen MC series.

Her first erotic book was written when she was thirteen. Of course, the most risqué thing was a kiss, but it was the talk of her middle school!

She is currently pursuing a doctoral degree in education and writes whenever she can. In her spare time, she enjoys dating, shopping, reading way too many romance novels, and drinking a truly obscene amount of coffee.

SHERI SAVILL

Slipknot

Sheri Savill is the author of dark BDSM erotic romance, and humor, and is a real-life submissive who was into BDSM before it was cool. A career in media and journalism (reporter, editor, DJ, copywriter) drove her to the brink of insanity, so she became an attorney and web developer.

Known for her irreverent blog, Savill is tattooed, pierced, geeky, easily annoyed yet fun-loving, and well caffeinated. She speaks often of a treasured "letter from Dave Barry" that no one has actually seen. Award-winning sex author and columnist Violet Blue called Savill's BDSM parody "painfully, hilariously timeless."

When she's not charging her portable electronic devices, Savill spends her time writing, thinking about writing, or wishing she had written. She scored a780 out of 800 on a standardized writing test of some sort and, just as she predicted, has never had to use calculus in her entire adult life.

SHOSHANNA EVERS

This Might Hurt A Bit

New York Times and USA Today Bestselling author Shoshanna Evers has written dozens of sexy stories. She is best known for The Enslaved Trilogy, The Tycoon's Convenient Bride…and Baby, Overheated, and How to Write Hot Sex. Evers is also the cofounder of SelfPub-BookCovers.com, the largest selection of premade book covers in the world. Reviewers have called Shoshanna's writing "sensuous, delightful, and sizzling" with stories where "the plot is fresh and the pacing excellent, the emotions…real and poignant." Shoshanna used to work as a syndicated advice columnist and a registered nurse, but now she's a full-time romance writer and a homeschooling mom. She lives with her family and three big dogs in Northern Idaho, and loves to connect with readers!

CANDY QUINN

The Bombshell

Candy loves writing naughty, nasty stories. Barely legal teens, sexy breeding stories, and misbehaving daddy's girls, all with the spiciest twists around. If you need something to scratch that secret itch, turn to Candy!

TAMSIN FLOWERS

Playing with Fire

Tamsin Flowers writes light-hearted erotica, often with a twist in the tail and a sense of fun. Her stories have appeared in numerous anthologies and usually, she's working on at least ten stories at once. While she figures out whose leg belongs in which story, you can find out more at Tamsin's Superotica.

ELIZABETH COLDWELL

Disposing of Donnie

Elizabeth Coldwell is a multi-published author and award-winning editor who lives and writes in London. Her work has appeared in a variety of anthologies including Crimes of Passion and Women With Handcuffs. She can be found at The (Really) Naughty Corner, elizabethcoldwell.wordpress.com.

AUDREY LUSK

Surprise Witness

Audrey Lusk has led a life that reads like fiction. As a voice actor, Audrey's performances of many steamy stories grace the Audible "shelves." And yet, for someone who spent time in modern burlesque, made and sold her own Goth clothing line, and ran professional murder mystery parties, she's a surprisingly evasive and retiring individual—and insists that these things found her, not the other way around. Now that she's finally found a way to make writing and recording her main focus, she plans to stick to it, averring triumphantly "I don't have to get dressed."

TRENT EVANS

Last Day

Trent Evans is an independent author of BDSM erotic romance and erotica. Putting pen to paper since he was a wee lad, he decided to try to share some of the tales cooked up in his fevered imagination. Some readers might not be horrified at what he writes. He tries to write stories that appeal to both women and men (wow, threading the needle), but will follow wherever the story takes him.

A long-time resident of the Pacific Northwest, the author believes that the high percentage of authors in the region (compared to the nation as a whole) is chiefly due to the fact that it's so damned wet and miserable all the time there. They tend to use their long hours cooped up inside spinning yarns that depict things they'll never see or experience—such as sunshine.

GISELLE RENARDE

Acquitted

Giselle Renarde is a queer Canadian, contributor to more than 100 short story anthologies, and award-winning author of juicy books like Anonymous, Cherry, Bali Nights, Nanny State, the Wedding Heat series and the Adam and Sheree trilogy. Giselle lives across from a park with two bilingual cats who sleep on her head.

ISBN: 9781501077692

TAKE THE HEAT

Copyright © 2014 by Skye Warren
Print Edition
Cover design by Book Beautiful

All rights reserved. Except for use in a review, the reproduction or use of this work in any part is forbidden without the express written permission of the author.

This is a work of fiction. Any resemblance to actual persons, living or dead, business establishments, events or locales is entirely coincidental. The author does not condone sexual acts without consent.

Printed in Poland
by Amazon Fulfillment
Poland Sp. z o.o., Wrocław